106 Arrowhead Drive

THE NEXT GENERATION

To God be the glory!
Kathy Highley

106 Arrowhead Drive

THE NEXT GENERATION

Kathleen Rigdon Highley

Copyright © 2017 by Kathleen Rigdon Highley.

ISBN:	Softcover	978-1-5434-4851-1
	eBook	978-1-5434-4852-8

All rights reserved. No part of this book may be reproduced or transmitted in any form or by any means, electronic or mechanical, including photocopying, recording, or by any information storage and retrieval system, without permission in writing from the copyright owner.

Scripture quotations marked NIV are taken from the Holy Bible, New International Version®. NIV®. Copyright © 1973, 1978, 1984 by International Bible Society. Used by permission of Zondervan. All rights reserved. [Biblica]

This is a work of fiction. Names, characters, places and incidents either are the product of the author's imagination or are used fictitiously, and any resemblance to any actual persons, living or dead, events, or locales is entirely coincidental.

Any people depicted in stock imagery provided by Thinkstock are models, and such images are being used for illustrative purposes only.
Certain stock imagery © Thinkstock.

Print information available on the last page.

Rev. date: 09/07/2017

To order additional copies of this book, contact:
Xlibris
1-888-795-4274
www.Xlibris.com
Orders@Xlibris.com
767066

In loving memory of my cherished mother, Rusti Sterling
9/5/35 - 7/24/17

Dedicated to the Promise my Lord gives me in Jeremiah 29:11-12
"For I know the plans I have for you," says the Lord. "Plans to prosper you and not to harm you. Plans to give you hope and a future. Then you will call on me and come and pray to me, and I will listen to you."

Don't always believe what you see.

Don't always believe what you hear.

But know this: God keeps His promises!

Anonymous

Chapter 1

When his time of service was completed, he returned home

(Luke 1:23 NIV).

MATTHEW BALDWIN approached the luggage carrier at the airport of his "hometown" of Lubbock, Texas. He'd been born there, and spent the first eight years of his life in Ransom Canyon, then his mother whisked the family away in the dead of night, running from a vindictive, vengeful, cruel grandmother. On occasion, the past came looming up at him like a big, black monster. Unresolved questions remained. Questions he'd run from all those years ago. And now he was headed right back into the throes of those dark memories.

He could do this. He'd faced much more harrowing events in Afghanistan. Dangers you could touch, and see, and hear, and smell.

What he had to face in Ransom Canyon, however, had been growing deep inside him like a tangle of seaweed wrapped around his heart.

But in spite of it all, Matt had grown to be a fine figure of a man, an honorable man who loved the Lord and his country with a passion experienced by a very small minority of the population. He'd been honorably discharged from the Navy six months earlier, but had taken some much needed time to deal with some particularly nasty war ghosts, visit the family of one of his fallen comrades—and to avoid the return home until the last possible moment. And now, with delayed flights here and there, he would barely make it to the house in time for his mother's wedding.

"Matt!"

Kimberly's voice invaded Matt's thoughts, and he searched the room for her face. Seconds later, Kim ran toward her big brother, a wide smile spread across her face.

"Hey, Kimmie."

Matt received Kim's long hug with a grateful heart. His baby sister had always been his favorite sibling, the only one out of five who had not spent any of her growing up years in the family estate, at 106 Arrowhead Drive, in Ransom Canyon. He stared at her now, a grown woman, beautiful and brilliant, a prosecuting attorney on her way up the proverbial ladder. She looked amazing. Even more amazing than the image that had looked back at him from the intermittent family photos his mother had managed to send over the years. His baby sister was far from being a baby, now.

"Come on, Matt! We'd better get cracking. As it is, we'll have to delay the ceremony while you get dressed."

"How about we wait till my luggage comes around," said Matt with a chuckle.

Eunice Mae Howell held the aging newspaper on her lap, her hands folded primly along the folded edge. A satisfied grin had not left her face in all the weeks since Kim's rescue. Her dream had, at last, come true. She, Maggie and Elizabeth had all made headline news. What a thrill. Kimberly was safe, and the family had the three oldest and bravest of the clan to thank for it.

Maggie had given up trying to convince Eunice Mae that life had returned to normal. That the espionage chapter had been closed. She told Eunice Mae she'd been tickled for her, though. Really. Eunice Mae Howell had believed with her whole heart that she and Maggie would nail Joe Maxwell for his crime, before the police or FBI had a clue. When it didn't work out that way, Eunice Mae had been more than a little disappointed. She had actually grieved. But she'd also been angry, and more determined than ever to find a way to get Joe Maxwell put behind bars, where he belonged.

Maggie and Eunice Mae had, however, discovered where Kimberly had been locked up, after Joe Maxwell's even more heinous crime of kidnapping. The discovery had been a God-send. Dear, courageous Eunice Mae would likely be content for the rest of her days. Maybe.

Eunice Mae Howell had flown with WASP in her younger days. A hero from WWII, envied by many women who had not had the opportunity to serve in such a capacity. And revered by those with whom she had served. Eunice Mae Howell had an adventurous streak that ran deep. Settling into a rocking chair for her golden years did not fit the profile.

Still, here she sat with a grin on her face that would be a challenge to erase. The wedding would take place in the very house Joe Maxwell had been hired to implode. The Baldwin Estate had been saved, and the family reunited. Maybe one day, Eunice Mae would see yet another adventure, equal to the task of warranting Eunice Mae's full attention. But for the moment, she seemed content.

The transformation of the house made it seem less like a museum for Catherine Baldwin. Old memories still lingered, and most of the antiques her deceased husband, Brad, had loved so well still remained. But the color scheme had been updated and the stuffed buzzard that sat on the hearth had been donated to the local Ombudsman Society. And good riddance. Catherine did not care for the strange, ugly treasure. She and Brad had never agreed on its significance to the decor. And now that the front room, dining room, kitchen, and staircase had been decorated for the wedding, even Brad's mother, Elizabeth, had agreed the buzzard had to go. Her son may have gone overboard with the Nature theme when he stuck that scavenger on the hearth, after all. Observing the transformation now, Catherine appreciated the house even more than before. The subtle change in color and content enhanced its beauty and brought a smile to the faces of those who had always admired its unique interior.

A pianist from the Lubbock Symphony Orchestra played quietly at the magnificent white Grand piano on the far side of the great room. Guests began to arrive. It wouldn't be long before Catherine would glide down the staircase in her cream-colored satin wedding gown. The simple but elegant lines had been cut to fit her still-small waistline and enhance her petite frame. The skirt gradually flared at the bottom to form a soft swirl at her feet. The creamy gown made a lovely contrast against the plush, new champagne carpeting. Catherine wore her grandmother's pearls above the rounded neck of the dress, and her mother's wedding band, to which Tommy would add his own mother's set.

A veil of cream-colored netting hung shoulder-length on all sides, while her golden hair, entwined in a long French braid, reached the middle of her back. A grandmother now, she had considered cutting it into a style befitting one of her age and station; but considering is not doing, so it remained long. After all, not one strand of gray had dared intrude on the shining tresses, and her youthful appearance contradicted her age. Princess style satin shoes, her life-long favorite, had been dyed to match her gown, and she wore Eunice Mae's anklet, for something borrowed.

As the guests filled the great room, seated in rows of white wrought-iron chairs with mauve satin cushions, Eunice Mae looked up to find Lucille, Catherine's neighbor, looking down at her. Eunice

Mae had seen Lucille at the Lubbock Country Club on occasion, but they associated with different sets of friends, and so had interacted very little.

"Excuse me," said Lucille, rather timidly. "Aren't you Eunice Mae Howell?"

"One and the same. And your name is Lucille, I believe."

"That's right. Lucille Mansfield. I live across the street and up one house. I can see that a wedding is about to take place here and I hate to interrupt, but I didn't know how soon I would get another opportunity to talk to you. Is there some place we could speak in private on a matter of great importance?"

What could be of greater importance than Catherine's wedding?

Eunice Mae glanced around the room then said, "Certainly. We still have a few minutes. I'll be right back," she whispered to Maggie as she slipped out the door.

Maggie nodded, placed Eunice Mae's newspaper in the seat she had vacated, and her purse in the one beyond it, just in case, then made her way across the room and up the stairs to wait with the wedding party. Eight minutes, and counting, to start time.

Eunice Mae led Lucille back out the front door and around to the north side of the house. The temperature still felt mild on this 20th day of June, for the sun had just begun to dry up the morning dew. The ladies stepped carefully along the stone path to keep their feet out of the grass.

"This should do nicely," said Eunice Mae. "What's on your mind, Lucille?"

"I owe you an apology. May I call you Eunice Mae?"

"Of course. But whatever could you owe me an apology for?"

"I'm afraid I was responsible for the police showing up the day you found Kim in the tool shed. You see, I've always been fascinated by this house, its history, and the people who lived here," Lucille went on to say. "I was here when Dr. Baldwin passed away and Mrs. Baldwin disappeared with the children. I can't tell you how much trouble I got into from my late husband when I would spend hours gazing out the window or observing the goings on from my front porch. Oh, I know it was tacky of me, but I just couldn't resist."

106 Arrowhead Drive had been the subject of several newspaper articles in and around Lubbock County through the years. Strangers had been known to drive by and snap pictures from the road. Dr. Baldwin and his family had become quite famous. The family had not been seeking notoriety, and would have much preferred their privacy. But it was not to be. Elizabeth Baldwin had used her considerable resources to make a spectacle of the family. Overcoming the aftermath had required tremendous effort.

Eunice Mae forced her mind to leave the memories and give her undivided attention to Lucille.

"I've been watching the house closely ever since," continued Lucille, "praying for the mother and her children. I've been praying for Elizabeth, as well. I've known Elizabeth since we were in grade school. That's why I called 911, twice. I wouldn't want Elizabeth's wrath to come down on my head, so I've managed to keep my identity out of the papers."

"I understand completely," said Eunice Mae, delighted. "Well, you'll be glad to know that Elizabeth came to know Christ as her personal Savior, and is truly a new creation. But tell me what you mean by calling 911, *twice*. What other time?"

"The day they arrested Joe Maxwell in front of the house," she answered.

"So that's what happened," said Eunice Mae. "I wondered who had tipped off the police. Just figured one of Joe's own kind had finally turned on him. How about that. Four old ladies helped bring Joe Maxwell's life of crime to a screeching halt. That's priceless," she said with pride, and a wide grin.

"Say, if you don't have any other plans, I'm inviting you to stay for the wedding. There's plenty of cake, and the mother of those five children is getting married today to Elizabeth's son-in-law, who was widowed by Elizabeth's daughter many years ago. Anyway, it's a long story. Maybe I'll tell it to you one of these days."

"Oh, I'd love that," squeaked Lucille, like she was a junior high student caught up in a stream of gossip. "Do you think I could get a tour of the house sometime?"

Eunice Mae smiled warmly at her new friend, with a confidence she had earned as an important "adopted" member of the Baldwin family, seeing as Maggie, their nanny, qualified as Eunice Mae's best friend and fellow adventurer.

"Oh sure. I'll see to it myself. I'm so glad you came over. This could be the start of a wonderful new friendship. And maybe you can help keep me and Maggie out of trouble," said Eunice Mae, with a conspiratorial wink.

The wedding party settled into place just as Eunice Mae and Lucille took their seats. Eunice Mae smiled with gratitude, knowing for sure that her friend Maggie had saved two seats, rather than one.

Maggie held a special place in the heart of Eunice Mae Howell. She had tolerated Eunice Mae's crazy adventures, even helped her a time or two. Maggie had a level head, and had tried to steer Eunice Mae down a path of safety and logic. But even when Eunice Mae didn't listen, Maggie stood by her friend to the bitter end. They had developed a mutual love and respect for one another, a fast bond that would hold for a lifetime. A big hole in Eunice Mae's heart had been filled with Maggie and the amazing family Maggie had been with since the age of twelve.

Eunice Mae observed the gathering, and tears filled her eyes at the wonder of it all. So much heartache, so much loss—totally transformed into so much joy, so much love.

Catherine and Tommy stood in front of the massive fireplace on the ground floor at 106 Arrowhead Drive in Ransom Canyon. Beaming, flanked on either side by Paul, the best man, James and Matt, groomsmen; and next to Catherine, Kimberly stood as Maid of

Honor (it seemed the least Catherine could do, since Kimberly had been the catalyst that had made it possible to return to their home), with Brooke and Maggie as bridesmaids. The men, decked out in elegant gray tuxedoes, stood proudly alongside the ladies in their stylish yet modest mauve-colored satin dresses and matching satin low-heeled shoes.

Elizabeth Baldwin sat in her wheelchair in the aisle of the front row next to her husband, Devin, their fingers entwined and resting on her lap. Jessica Roberts sat behind them with her mother Marilyn; and Eunice Mae couldn't help but notice that Matt couldn't help but notice Jessica.

The wheels began to turn, and Eunice Mae Howell pictured a whole new generation coming up behind them. She believed in her heart, the house would live on for many generations to come—alive with children, and grandchildren, and great grandchildren.

Chapter 2

At the right time, I, the Lord, will make it happen (Isaiah 60:22 NLT).

JESSICA stole a glance in Matt's direction as they stepped out into the sun. A smile spread across her face as he glanced her way; but he immediately turned back to watch his mother. He didn't look disinterested, necessarily, just distracted. Jessica was glad he wasn't staring back at her, for her gaze lingered, as though a celebrity had joined them. Her heart skipped a beat. A more handsome man she had never seen. He towered over his brothers, stretching to at least six foot, five inches. He had been separated from the Navy long enough for his hair to hang over his shirt collar and most of his ear. My stars, he's gorgeous, she thought. He had inherited his mother's golden mane and chocolate brown eyes, his father's full lips, and his grandfather's impressive physique.

What sort of man occupied that body, that mind, thought Jessica. What ruled his heart, his decisions, his motivation? No one in the family had seen him since he'd graduated high school. And only Kim and Catherine had received so much as a post card from him during his twelve-year absence, which included six years' active duty as a naval aviator. Jessica knew that, because she and Kim had remained fast friends through college, and beyond. Mostly.

A cloud rolled in and hid the sun for a moment, casting a soft hue over the crowd gathered in front of the house. A slight breeze brought a measure of relief from the hot, dry June day that had warmed up in a hurry. Jessica glanced up and smiled, grateful for the reprieve. But when she looked back over the crowd, she almost choked on her breath mint. Matt Baldwin caught her eye, winked at her, and offered a captivating grin. Temporarily stunned, Jessica looked down at the sidewalk, unsure what to think, or do. When she raised her head, Matt had moved toward the limo that waited to take his mother and Tommy to the airport, bound for the Dallas International Airport then on to a 10-day river cruise through Italy.

Jessica found herself intrigued by this mysterious man, who now smiled openly at his mother. As Jessica watched, Catherine stood on tiptoe and received a hug from her son, the glimmer of a tear on her cheek. Made sense. Catherine hadn't seen her son for more than twelve years—only to tell him goodbye again. Almost immediately.

Twelve years, with only a few postcards to show for his long absence. Kim had shared the contents with Jessica, who had shown the interest due a friend. But the man who stood across the way at this moment seemed more rich and vibrant than the one-dimensional words on a two-by-two square.

Jessica made herself look away then joined Kim. It was good to see her again. Their college years had been fun, and special. But Kim had drifted after that. The boyfriends had changed in a lot of ways. Law school students seemed more intense, more stressed, more liberal. Jessica had been concerned about Kim, more than once. In her first year of law school, Kim had fallen for half a dozen guys. And been totally heartbroken, every time. Each new love interest had come from a more wealthy family than the one before. Some of them had come from foreign countries and imposed foreign ideas on Kim. Praise God, none of the strange notions had taken root. They could at least be grateful that Jessica had not slipped off the Christian foundation that had been laid early in her life. But Kim did seem confused, and a little lost, still groping for that missing piece that would make her feel whole.

Still searching, still unsure of who she was or wanted to be, Kim eloped to Las Vegas during her third year of law school, with a man who turned out to be a self-centered, egotistical, crazy person who gave her a black eye on more than one occasion—until Kim's family banded together, kidnapped her from her home, and stood beside her until the divorce was final. Kim's ex-husband moved to Houston after the divorce, where he joined a law firm that had made the jerk a ridiculous offer. Kim rallied, finished law school, joined a local law firm, took to the work like she was born to prosecute. She thrived in the legal field, and built a reputation for efficiency, thoroughness, honesty, and a thick skin. A female in her field had to be tough. Even so, the empty place she believed could be filled only with the loyal love of a man, continued to grow, and six months later, Kim was in love again.

Jessica had tried to talk sense into Kimberly on romantic issues, but to no avail. She had even suggested counseling, but the inference had not been well received. There had to be a reason, buried deep inside Kim, that kept her going from man to man with very little filter to help avoid repeating the same error, over and over again. Jessica's ideas on just how to do that had been shut down with little or no consideration. Therefore, she simply didn't go there anymore.

Jessica had promised to drop the subject of Kimberly's romantic relationships, and she'd kept her promise. But it had taken a concentrated effort to keep her mouth shut. Rather, she would relish the special moments they shared, like today, when the obvious topic would be obvious, and Kim's love life wasn't likely to come up.

Kim would have other personal feelings to deal with today, anyway. Matt, her favorite brother, had finally made an appearance, after being gone from home since the day after high school graduation. Kim practically idolized Matthew. They had been close all her life. Matt had dragged Kim around with him from the time she could barely walk till Matt left home. She had her first taste of ice cream with Matt holding the waffle cone. He had introduced her to its mint chocolate chip goodness, with no apology. Kim had once confessed that she'd been a passenger on Matt's motorcycle at the tender age of five, a secret they believed they had successfully kept from their mother, to this day.

Jessica certainly didn't know all of Kim's secrets, and knew very little about Matt, the man. But her heart told her she wanted to know more. Maybe a relationship with Matthew Baldwin would give her more opportunity to influence Kim. Or maybe her big brother would be able to soothe Kim's disquieted spirit, and Jessica's best friend would once again stand on solid ground.

Matthew Bradley Baldwin stood straight and tall, his hand shading the sun, as he watched his mother ride away in the back of a long, lavender limousine. She had smiled up into his face, tears glistening, and silently forgiven him. The words had not passed her lips, but he knew. And one day he would thank her.

Matt surveyed the landscape that surrounded him; and sudden, unwelcome darkness flooded his soul. His last memory of 106 Arrowhead Drive had been from the back seat of his mother's Suburban, in the middle of the night, at the ripe old age of eight. He had stared out the side window, silently, as tears wet his face, dripped off his chin, and soaked the pillow Maggie had brought with her from his bed. He knew his father had died, but it would be a long while before he knew the truth behind their clandestine escape.

As the limo disappeared from view, Matt felt someone alongside him. A hand touched his elbow and he knew before he looked down. Maggie. She had known him better than any adult in his life.

"You okay?"

He smiled.

"Better now, thanks," he said, making eye contact. "I was just thinking about the last time I was here. Sometimes it still hurts."

Maggie squeezed his elbow.

"Maybe while you're home, you can get some form of closure. Look how much good it has done Kim to face the past. To not let go till she had the answers she came looking for. She's better, for the most part anyway."

"What do you mean 'for the most part'?"

"Forget I said anything. We don't need to talk about anything heavy today. We'll get together one day while you're here, and I'll tell you all I know. Together, I believe we can make a difference for Kimmie."

"It's a date. Maybe I'll get a chance to talk to her in private."

"And hopefully, she'll talk to you. Lately, even Jessica hasn't been able to crack that thick shell of hers."

"Thanks for the heads-up. I'd covet your prayers for the both of us, Maggie."

"Done."

Matthew frowned at the news Maggie had shared with him. What had happened to change his baby sister from a sweet, happy child into an adult with unresolved issues? He knew from the letters he'd received that Kim had married and divorced inside two years of the wedding. Kim had not disclosed why, but his mother's letters had expressed concern for Kim's well-being, and had asked for prayer on her behalf. Kim's choices could bring consequences she might not have considered. Even Catherine's information had been vague, so Matt still had no idea what had been troubling his baby sister. Attorney or no, Kimmie would always be his baby sister.

Matt forced thoughts of Kim to the back of his mind, and surveyed the old neighborhood. It didn't look much different than he remembered. The same regal homes graced the same spacious, well-manicured lots. The slope of Arrowhead Drive remained the same. The grass still sported the same rich shade of green, and the sun still set on the same side of the hill. For Matt, the eight years he had lived and played there had been nothing less than glorious.

As the limo curved to the right at the bottom of the hill, Matt and Maggie turned back toward the house. The family stood in the front yard, all of them staring after the limousine. It seemed as though they hung in limbo, waiting for some magic bubble to burst.

Catherine Baldwin had become Catherine Baldwin-Churchwell that day. Each child of hers had their own set of memories when it came to her new husband, Tommy Churchwell. And they each respected him. He had kept his relationship with their mother on a back burner until they had all grown up. Every last one of them. Out of respect for their father. He had not pushed himself on any of them; but made it clear, he would be available if any of them might need him, for anything, at any time.

Matt remembered the night he followed Tommy home, after the third Thanksgiving he'd spent with them in Tennessee. They stood in front of Tommy's mother's house, on an unseasonably warm Thursday evening.

"I know you like my mother," said Matt.

"Yes, I do," said Tommy. "I like all of you."

"You know what I mean."

"Yes, yes, I believe I do," said Tommy, thoughtful, respectful. "Let's sit here on the swing for a minute. I'll tell you anything you want to know, so long as it is my place to reveal."

Tommy had confided in Matt that night. He had gone all the way back to elementary school, and through his college years. He had explained that he'd married Alexis Baldwin to give her baby a name. Another man's baby. Then stood by, silently, as Catherine, the only true love of his life, married his brother-in-law.

Matt had carried the burden, as well as the privilege, of knowing the truth, from that day, till this. He didn't know whether his brothers and sisters knew the whole story. He had spoken of it to no one. Just as Matt had never talked about the death of his father, a man he had loved with the trust of a child. A man who had worked a lot of hours, saved countless lives, and still managed to be there for his family, each one of them, whenever they needed him, or just wanted to be with him, or wrestle with him, or hear him read to them. He had taken them to church, prayed with them, and played with them.

Then one day, he was gone. Forever. His life cut short by a brain aneurysm that exploded and took Dr. Bradley Devin Baldwin III out of the picture.

Three weeks after the funeral, the family left 106 Arrowhead Drive, and life as Matt had known it, behind.

Now, at age 30, he had been to several countries, experienced multiple cultures and terrains, and had once come close to falling in love, but not quite. True to his nature, Matt had been restless and non-committal. And today, once again, Matt found himself on the turf his family had run away from so many years ago.

Decisions would have to be made. The past would one day need to be dealt with.

But not today.

Today, he would catch up with his brothers and sisters, hug his mother's mother, affectionately known as Grammi, treasure this time with Maggie, cautiously approach Grandmother Baldwin, whom he would have to learn to trust—and make sure Kimberly introduced him to Jessica Roberts.

The appeal had been undeniable. On any given day, Matt Baldwin preferred brunettes with long, straight hair. But this girl—this Jessica—struck a nerve.

She seemed to be a living portrait of the personality Kim had painted of a saucy photo journalist in her letters. Her chin-length, beyond-blonde, hair bounced with her every movement. The twinkle in those unique, can't-tell-if-they're-green-or-blue eyes, danced with mirth and held a sparkle, a silent challenge, that spoke to his restless spirit.

Kim approached her big brother with a well-earned confidence. She knew him better than any of the siblings, better than even he might guess.

"Let me introduce you," she said with a grin.

Kim glanced at Maggie as she shuffled off, pretty sure why she made herself scarce. Eunice Mae had told both of them that she had picked up on the attraction between Matt and Jessica earlier in the day. Helping them get together would be well received by the family. After all, it was high time Matt settled down and planted himself in one spot. He just needed a little push in the right direction. Never mind about her own misguided decisions in that regard. She could plainly see what was best for Matt, best for her long-time good friend, Jessica Roberts.

"What are you talking about?"

Kim simply laughed, looped her arm through his, and guided him toward Jessica.

"I don't believe you've met my brother," said Kim. "Since he barely made it here in time for the ceremony."

"Ha ha," said Matt. "I had no control over flight delays."

"Nice to meet you," said Jessica, extending her hand. "I know your mother is pleased you could make it."

Matt wrapped his large hand around Jessica's smaller one. Their eyes met, and held for several seconds.

"The pleasure is all mine," said Matt.

Kim felt her heart swell. This could work. Her best friend and her favorite brother. Yes, this could work out nicely for all of them. And would definitely give her family something to talk about that had nothing to do with Kim's current infatuation. Or the next. Or the one after that.

Chapter 3

Precious in the sight of the Lord is the death of his faithful servants
(Psalm 116:15 NIV).

TWENTY-FOUR hours later, over salad and pizza, the Baldwin siblings sat around the dining room table of their childhood home.

"Okay, big guy," said Paul, the oldest brother. "What kind of crazy adventure have you been on? And why have you been so silent? Did you join the Foreign Legion or something?"

Matt chuckled. Crazy adventure. Paul's idea of a crazy adventure amounted to a camp-out with two adults for every seven kids. Matt's life had been much, much different.

While his siblings ragged on him about being gone too long and keeping out of touch, Matt's mind took him back to one of his favorite Navy memories...

"Look, Matthew," said Captain Barton. "I get it. You want to see real action. Itching to be in the thick of things."

Captain Barton had spoken the truth. Matthew Bradley Baldwin had been a naval aviator for close to two years, and had yet to come face-to-face with the enemy. The Navy called it Deterrence Missions—an unquestioned power, an aircraft carrier strategically on station, to discourage aggression. He knew he was helping, knew that every man who served in any capacity, was helping to make a difference. But Matt wanted to battle the enemy in a more intimate way. He wanted to *see* the difference he was making; wanted to count, first-hand, the crash-and-burn tally. To know for sure, *that* one would not be back to kill another American serviceman.

"I won't deny it," said Matt. "You know as well as I do, the Navy could park anyone out here in this part of the ocean to keep things from heating up. I understand that; and I've been here long enough. Now, about that transfer request."

Captain Barton had come aboard for the express purpose of offering Matt a live mission, as well as a promotion to Lieutenant. At least that's what Matt had hoped for when he had been called to the cabin of his superior officer.

"A transfer could be a plausible answer to your dilemma," said Captain Barton. "And what I am here to offer you might be considered a transfer, but."

"But what, sir?"

"The Navy has kept an eye on you ever since you graduated from the Academy. You have skills, and character, and integrity, but you're also reckless and careless with your own life. You take unnecessary risks."

Matt couldn't argue the fact. But he didn't consider his life in danger when he was at the controls. He knew what he was doing, what he was thinking. He could not change the opinion of anyone else, or convince them of the fact. But that didn't make it any less true.

"However," Captain Barton continued. "We believe your potential can be harnessed into an even greater service to your country than you have already performed."

"How so?"

"What would you say to manning a Super Fudd? I'm sure you're familiar with the E-2 Hawkeye's rotating radar capability. And the fact that it can track low-lying aircraft from some 250 miles out. Interested?"

Matt suppressed a grin. Of course he'd heard about the Northrop Grumman twin turbo prop defensive aircraft. Getting into the cockpit would be a dream come true.

"The assignment also comes with a promotion," added Barton.

"When do I leave?"

Matt had heard the captain's words. The promotion didn't interest him as much as the assignment. The assignment had him intrigued. The current E-2C models were playing an essential role in the Middle East, launching from the USS *George Bush* to serve as flying command posts and air traffic control for the ongoing strikes against the self-proclaimed Islamic State. You bet he was willing to go.

"Tomorrow morning," said Captain Barton. "Training begins in 48 hours."

"By your standards," said Matt with a chuckle, as he returned to the present, "I've been on one long crazy adventure since I turned ten."

Paul laughed. "This is true. But really, what have you been up to? You are our brother, and we care about you."

James nodded in agreement. And Brooke reached across the table to rest her hand on Matt's forearm.

"He's right, Matt. I wish you had kept in touch better."

Matt raised his hands in surrender.

"You're probably right," he said. "But I have kept in touch. Isn't that right, Kimmie?"

"It's true," she said.

"There you go," said Matt. "Sometimes you only have time for one postcard."

"Fair enough," said Paul. "I won't pester you about it. But it's hard to get to know a person through two or three lines on a postcard. Especially since I only saw a few of them. Why don't you tell us about yourself. For instance, is there a special girl?"

A picture of Jessica Roberts flashed through his mind. Unbidden, but clear.

"Uh, not at the moment. And as for the rest, I'll fill you in someday. But right now, I'd just like to enjoy being home, and finish my pizza."

"Same old Matt," said James.

They all knew what "same old Matt" meant. He had grown increasingly introverted and reckless since they'd moved to Nashville. Matt knew it, too. But nothing had happened through the years that had given him any urge to change. He had locked up the demons and focused on his career. Now, with the Navy behind him, he would have to figure out what to do with the rest of his life.

Three days after the wedding, Jessica stood on the doorstep in front of her house, and stared.

"At least you didn't laugh," said Matt.

With his words, she couldn't hold it back any longer. She laughed with abandon.

"I'm sorry," she finally said. "I'm just surprised, is all. Doesn't fit the legendary image."

"If you'll still go out with me, I'll tell you all about it."

"I wouldn't miss it."

As Jessica settled into the front seat of the shiny, cranberry red 1956 Cadillac convertible, she looked around. Not a speck of dust on the dash, not a single ball of fuzz on the still-plush carpet. Immaculate. How could that be? This car had to be pushing sixty, yet looked like it just rolled off the showroom floor.

She could hardly hold in the question, and waited for Matt to position himself behind the wheel of the oversized tank of an automobile.

"Where would you like to have dinner?" he said, flashing a grin her way.

"Oh no you don't," said Jessica. "I want the story. Supper can wait."

Matt took his hands off the wheel and turned to face his date.

"No big mystery really," he said. "My grandfather on my mother's side bought this car brand new. It then spent most of its life pampered and treasured, in his garage."

"How did you?"

"Not a trick there either. I'm the only child who wanted it. Sounds nuts, I know. My siblings must be a little off balance. Besides, I really like the leg room. And to be honest, I'm the only mechanically-inclined brother."

Jessica joined Matt in a hearty laugh. She loved the sound of it. Kim had shared small bits of Matt's story with her; and the relaxed man she saw before her seemed far removed from the tales of adventure and mischief she'd heard about. Which enhanced the intrigue all the more.

Oh yes. Jessica Roberts very much wanted to get to know Matthew Baldwin.

For the third day in a row, the third week in a row, the sun came up—unbidden and unwelcome. Life seemed much more simple in a dream. Boy meets girl, falls in love, encounters little or no resistance; they marry, have two and one-half children, purchase a house with a yard surrounded by a white picket fence, acquire a dog, and live happily ever after.

This would not be the first time a dream had not become reality for Jessica Roberts. Or so it would seem at this juncture. For Matt Baldwin had not called or darkened her doorway over the long, barren stretch of two weeks, and more. By now, Jessica had begun to doubt any potential relationship with Matt Baldwin. It had been their second date. Why did she expect so much, so soon?

I shouldn't have tried to kiss him. I knew it. But he was right there, just inches away, and so handsome. Those intriguing chocolate brown eyes had beckoned me, and I couldn't stop myself.

"He did kiss me back, though. I did not imagine that."

The excuses and the reality of a beautiful evening together, however memorable, could not erase the fact that Jessica had not seen or heard from Matt since he'd left her at the door, late on a Thursday night, July 4, after the fireworks display down by the lake in Ransom Canyon. He had told her that his dad had taken the kids every year. She had seen tears in his eyes, and wanted to console him. But the minute she opened her mouth to say so, he changed the subject. Like a faucet, he turned off the waterworks and turned his attention back to the show.

And that was the last she had seen of Matthew Baldwin. She may have regretted kissing him, if she had known it would mean he would disappear on her. But her heart did not regret the gesture, at the time.

"Oh well. Chalk it up to experience, and go on," she whispered.

She slipped into her shoes and headed out the door. Work beckoned, and she must answer its call.

The wind whipped his hair beneath the aerodynamic helmet as Matt Baldwin picked up speed. The Harley that roared beneath him helped him feel grounded, connected, and at the same time, free. He had, of late, felt a bit disjointed. He had been back in Ransom Canyon for about eight weeks, and the only adventure he'd had so far consisted of two trips to the lake to ski with one of Tommy's friends, a client who raised Great Danes. For fun. Fortunately, the man had a large ranch near a large body of water and a very large kennel under massive shade trees he had planted and nurtured for just such a purpose. Great Danes. Matt had never seen so much dog food in one location.

And then there was that one special date with Jessica. They had gone to dinner and then to the lake to watch the fireworks display, with about fifty other people. Unlike their pizza date shortly after the wedding—on fireworks night, she had kissed him.

That one kiss had done him in. A kiss so sweet and innocent it made his head spin. Now, he couldn't get Jessica out of his mind or his heart. It wouldn't take much of a shove to push him over the line, and deep into the love pit. He liked Jessica Roberts. Liked her a lot. And fear sent him on yet another road trip. The V-rod didn't make demands, didn't ask questions, or try to pin him down. He could soar down the long, lonely stretch of road, and shout into the wind, with no repercussions.

What did he need with Jessica Roberts anyway? He had no definite plan for his own future, and did not feel the need to complicate his life with the responsibility of another human being. He'd been free a long time, and liked it that way. Or so he thought. He found himself beginning to wonder what it would be like to see her every day, to hear the beautiful lilt of her voice across the table from him every morning and every evening.

Maybe it had been her eyes, or the feel of her lips on his, or the aloof way she'd treated him—until the kiss—that had drawn him to her. He really couldn't say. He'd been certain she would call him—most women from his past had pestered him beyond endurance. But Jessica hadn't called, or sent a text message, or even an e-mail. He couldn't speculate as to her feelings, but a big part of him wanted to find out one of these days—because Jessica Roberts intrigued him. Something deep inside Matt had been stirred up; something heretofore undisturbed.

Matt Baldwin throttled down, and challenged the 112 hp to do its best work. Surely, all thought of Jessica Roberts would be drowned in the guttural cry of the engine, as it carried him farther and farther out of the city limits.

"Is that you, Matt?" called Catherine, from the kitchen.

"Yes, ma'am."

Matt hung his leather jacket on the rack by the front door, and set his helmet on the shelf beneath it. He ran his fingers through his hair and wiped his brow with the sleeve of his shirt then joined his mother in the kitchen.

"Need me to reach something for you?"

Matt had been reaching things for his mother since the seventh grade. It was a natural question.

"Not this time," she said. "I really just wanted to talk. Got a minute?"

"Sure."

"Well, have a seat. Would you like a glass of tea?"

"Sounds good. I've just come off a long ride, and I'm a little parched."

"Hungry?"

"Not so much. Got any fruit?"

"Apples, oranges, bananas and blackberries."

"I think an apple, with a little cheese?"

"The apples are in the bowl on the table in the breakfast nook. I'll join you, soon as I grab some cheese and pour up some tea."

"Thanks, Mom."

Matt didn't feel much anxiety about what his mother might have on her mind. She probably just wanted a few minutes to catch up on the latest in his life. Catherine walked up beside him and set a tall glass of iced tea in front of him, along with a saucer covered in sliced cheddar cheese, his favorite. She took the seat across from him, and slowly began to peel the orange she had brought with her. She did not look up for a full minute.

"What's going on, Mom? Do you have bad news?"

Catherine raised her head, tears shining in her eyes.

"What's happened?" said Matt, a frown bringing his brows together. "Something happen to Tommy or one of the kids?"

"No, no. Tommy's fine. Your brothers and sisters are okay, too, so far as I know." She stopped to press a tissue under each eye.

"Mom."

"I'm sorry," she said. "It's Maggie. I found her this morning. The doctor said she had a massive heart attack in the night. I couldn't reach you on your cell, so I just waited until you came in."

Matt felt stunned. Maggie had been an icon in their family for three generations. She had been a mere child when the family had taken her in.

He had heard the story many times.

Catherine's parents had been on a mission trip to Brazil seven months before Catherine's birth. They had been going door-to-door with an interpreter when they spotted a young child, perhaps ten years of age, seated on a curb just ahead of them, crying. Weeping, her hands covering her face, her little shoulders trembling.

Mark approached the child, knelt down in front of her, and asked, "What's wrong, sweetie?"

With big chocolate eyes, the little girl peeked over her hands at the stranger with a blank look on her face. Mark glanced up at the interpreter. Juan hurried forward to help.

"Yes, Señor."

"Please ask her why she is crying."

Juan spoke to the young girl with tenderness in his voice. She answered quietly, as she wiped tears from her little face. Juan gave her a gentle hug then turned to face Mark.

"Her parents have been killed, and the other family members have turned her away. They say she is defective and must be cursed."

Red tape and a long wait followed. But two years later, Margaret Benita Ruiz came to live with her new guardians, Mark and Victoria Somersby. Juan the interpreter had kept in touch with Margaret and the nuns who had taken her in, while they waited.

From the moment little Maggie arrived, she had been family. Maggie took it upon herself to help with all household chores and to help care for baby Catherine. As missionary-minded parents to begin with, making homeschooling and ESL part of the daily routine had gone relatively smoothly. Margaret soon transitioned into Maggie, and seemed happy with her new family. Just what Maggie's family meant by labeling her defective did not become clear until a few weeks after Maggie moved in with the Somersby family.

Maggie had taken Catherine into the back yard to play so Victoria could get caught up on some paperwork. Thirty minutes had gone by when Victoria glanced out to check on the girls. She jumped up in alarm when she saw Maggie lying still on the ground, and Catherine standing over her, crying. Victoria dropped her pencil and raced out into the yard.

"Maggie! Maggie!" she cried. Victoria knelt beside Maggie and felt for a pulse. It was detectable, but faint. She grabbed up Catherine and raced back into the house, where she called Catherine's pediatrician, who advised her to call an ambulance and get Maggie to the hospital. She then called Mark then ran back out to stay with Maggie.

Finding out the truth added a new challenge to the Somersby family. Maggie had been born with an enlarged heart. By miraculous design, Maggie had survived, undiagnosed and untreated, until God maneuvered circumstances to insure she would be taken in by a godly family, who would love her and see to her proper care. Then, for the rest of her life, she lived medicated and on what some would call borrowed time.

Then that fateful night, Maggie succumbed at the relatively young age of sixty-nine, also a miracle of God's design. Maggie had given back at least what she had received, loved and been loved, and had repeatedly said she wouldn't change a thing. Not one, single, solitary thing about the life she had lived with the Somersby family, the Baldwin family, and finally, the Churchwell family.

Maggie. Matt would certainly miss Maggie. On some level, she seemed to understand his restlessness. She had encouraged his mother to take the plunge and purchase his first dirt bike. He'd been a kid, maybe ten years old. And Maggie had been the buffer between himself and everyone else during his turbulent teens. He had even gone so far, in his head, to think she might be the one person he could open up to about the loss of his father—an ache that still burned in his heart. And they had not had the talk about Kim, either. A twinge of guilt pricked his heart. Maggie would not have voiced concern for his baby sister without good reason.

But here he was, thinking about his own selfish needs, his own guilt, while his mother had lost a pillar in her life, too. Maggie. Dear, sweet, straightforward, stalwart-to-the-end, Maggie.

Matt stood, pulled the chair out between himself and his mother, dragged it closer and sat down, facing her. He rested his arms on his thighs and opened his hands, palms up.

"I'm so sorry," he said. "I know how special she was to you."

Catherine popped a Wet One out of the container behind the fruit bowl and wiped the orange from her hands then reached out to him. She smiled the tiniest bit.

"I know how special she was to you, too," she said. "Don't think I don't know all the mischief she tried to get you out of. I had my sources, you know."

"True," said Matt, not entirely surprised. "I will miss her very, very much."

Matt stood and opened his arms to his mother. She stepped into his embrace and began to cry. Big, brave, bold Matthew Baldwin joined her, and shed a tear for his old friend and nanny. Saying goodbye would not be easy.

Chapter 4

Is not wisdom found among the aged? Does not long life bring understanding? (Job 12:12 NIV)

The morning of August 21st, the Baldwin family, the Churchwells, and a few close friends gathered at 106 Arrowhead Drive, following a memorial service for Margaret Benita Ruiz. Every room of the house echoed stories of her presence. Every child she had nurtured under that roof had seen her lean far out over the second story landing, and call them by their full names: Paul Adam Baldwin; James Bartholomew Baldwin; Catherine Brooke Baldwin; Matthew Bradley Baldwin.

Only baby Kimberly Margaret Baldwin had escaped said tongue-lashing. For baby Kim had been a mere two weeks old when they left the Baldwin home behind. And being a soft-hearted person to begin with, Maggie had been unable to scold Kimberly for anything, ever. She had lost her father, and been raised in a foreign land (Tennessee), and that had been reason enough for Maggie to go easy on Kimberly Margaret. Maggie knew the pain of losing a parent, had lived it. And being her namesake, only added to Maggie's resolve to protect Kimberly. From everything and everybody.

Laughter, teasing, and tears filled the afternoon as friends and family reminisced about the life of their precious Maggie.

Eunice Mae Howell sat with the family at the memorial service and now joined in the chatter, covering the life of her dearest friend, until the sun hung low in the sky.

Maggie had met Eunice Mae on a mild but sunny May afternoon in the golf shop at the country club, when Maggie had taken Paul for a golf lesson, a gift for his seventh birthday. Although twenty years separated their ages, an instant camaraderie had formed during the hour they'd visited while waiting for Paul. Week after week they would spend that hour together. Maggie soon knew a great deal about Eunice Mae's life story, and Eunice Mae had sat spellbound as Maggie described her young life in Brazil in the midst of a drug-infested neighborhood, the mysterious fainting spells that no one took the time to have diagnosed, and the ultimate, almost predictable death of her parents in a drug deal gone bad. The Somersby family had saved Maggie from a fate worse than death. For although her extended family had no desire to nurture, love, and raise her, Maggie would have been a commodity in the sex-for-hire nightmare that would have put money in their pockets; and in light of her undiagnosed heart condition, would more than likely have meant an insufferable life, as well as a premature death.

Eunice Mae and Maggie began to expand their friendship. Eunice Mae introduced Maggie to plays and art and yachting, and a myriad of other social activities that had been second nature to Eunice for most of her life. From the culture and finery forced upon her from toddlerhood to the unique tastes Eunice Mae had developed on her own, they became fast friends.

A lovely, brave, and loving woman had died too soon. Eunice Mae would miss their talks and outings. Their philosophical and theological discussions. Their shared nights at the symphony and strolls through Frank Higginbotham Park. Yes, Eunice Mae would miss Maggie Ruiz. But just as Eunice Mae had carried on after the loss of so many loved ones before, she would carry on now. A little more every year, Eunice Mae became increasingly aware of her own immortality. At this rate, she would be greeted by a large host of friends and loved ones when she made her own appearance at the gates of heaven.

"I hate to bring this camaraderie to an end," said Eunice Mae, pulling herself back to the present. "But I am exhausted, and feel I must be getting home. Emotional exertion seems to be more tiring than physical labor." Eunice Mae dabbed a hanky delicately below each eye then turned toward Matt.

"Matthew, would you please see me home?"

"Of course." Anything for Maggie's best friend.

"And I'd like Jessica to come along for the ride," she continued.

"Jessica?"

"Yes, Jessica."

"Yes, ma'am, if that is what you wish."

"It is."

Eunice Mae Howell, still young at the age of 90, had a habit of commanding most any situation she found herself in. Strong-willed and confident in her convictions, people took her as she was, or didn't take her at all. She didn't concern herself with it, one way or another. She cared about all sorts of people; but it didn't bother her when her feelings were not reciprocated. She had grown beyond that, pushed to the edge following the loss of any close family relationship she had ever enjoyed—before the war. Before she removed herself from the societal circle she had been raised in—to become a "Rosie the Riveter", then on to join WASP as a pilot, designated to traffic airplanes from post to post, in order to free up men to leave the U.S. and engage in war. Her rebellion had not set well with the high-society-southern-belle-image her mother had worked hard to instill in her daughter.

Eunice Mae and Maggie became fast friends soon after Eunice Mae settled in Lubbock. And Maggie's connection with the Baldwin family automatically gave Eunice Mae a place in their family. A tight bond had formed between them all. Therefore, Eunice Mae could be considered more an aunt than an acquaintance.

No one questioned Eunice Mae's interest in Jessica Roberts. Maybe she simply wanted to get to know her better. Maybe she had an ulterior motive for inviting Jessica to ride with them. Maybe not. But it didn't matter. If Eunice Mae invited Jessica, everyone knew Jessica would join them.

Jessica asked Matt, "Should I ask Mother to wait here?"

"No need," said Marilyn. "I was just about to leave anyway. It's getting late, and tomorrow will come early. Would you mind taking Jessica to her place after you see Ms. Eunice safely home? It'll save me waiting here for her, and I'll go on to bed."

"Mother."

"It's no problem," said Matt. "I don't mind in the least."

He winked at Jessica, who turned swiftly away.

Oh well. Maybe she'll calm down—if I behave myself.

But Matt didn't exactly feel hopeful, considering his past history with relationships, not to mention the fact that he had willingly kissed Jessica on their date a few weeks back, then not called her. If he'd had no intention of ever seeing her again, the polite thing would be to excuse himself with dignity. But Matt had been pretty certain he did want to see Jessica again. Maybe, with a little finesse, he could work his way back into her good graces.

Matt held the front door of his Cadillac open for Eunice Mae. She declined the offer.

"I'd be more comfortable in the back seat," she said.

Matt glanced at Jessica, with brows raised. Jessica simply shrugged.

Matt knew better than to argue with Ms. Eunice, so he reached for the wide, white, leather-clad seat, and pulled it back. Eunice wriggled her way into the back.

"Thank you, dear."

"Yes, ma'am."

Matt stepped back just far enough to hold the door open for Jessica.

"Thank you, dear," whispered Jessica, clearly using Eunice Mae's Southern drawl, as she moved past him.

"Ha ha," he said, hope rising again with her expression of sarcastic humor.

Atta girl.

Matt drove the speed limit, and left the top up, at Eunice Mae's request. She had made it clear she was not a fan of the night air. Said she might catch her death of a cold.

"I know I've said it already, Ms. Eunice," said Matt, glancing in the rearview mirror, "but I'm so sorry you had to say goodbye to your friend."

"I appreciate that, sweetie. I'll miss that girl. The twenty years that spanned our ages didn't mean a thing. We became friends almost immediately. We identified with each other, since we had both been rejected by our families. There will be a big gaping hole in my life without Maggie. She helped keep me focused and my feet on the ground, if you know what I mean."

"Oh, I know," said Matt with a laugh. "Kim told me all about your big adventure to catch the bad guy."

Eunice Mae chuckled.

"One of the greatest adventures of my life. And I've had some doozies, let me tell you."

"I remember that story," said Jessica, turning sideways in the seat, so she could look Eunice Mae in the eye. "I was still in college, remember? Kim and I got in a lot of trouble over that house."

"Of course I remember. Very brave of you."

"I'd love to interview you about some of your other adventures," said Jessica. "I think your life would make a great human interest story."

"That's sweet of you, dear. But I am far too old for anyone to care about my adventures."

"Oh no, ma'am. Quite the contrary. You've lived a long, full life, and I *guarantee* people would love to read about it. Promise me you'll give it some thought. Please."

"That much I will promise," said Eunice Mae. "Might be fun. I suppose sharing my adventures could be an adventure in itself."

Jessica could hardly contain herself. The photo journalist in her had only grown more intense over the past few years, while working for the *Avalanche Journal*. She had even landed some independent work for *Time* magazine. A few weeks before Matt came home to Ransom Canyon, she had returned from Hong Kong, where she had covered the life of a WWII war veteran, who had settled in Hong

Kong, with the woman he had fallen in love with during the war. So, the story she longed to share regarding the adventures of Eunice Mae Howell fell right in line with her heart.

Jessica had begun to build a reputation in her own right. Matt's mother had revealed a small piece of Eunice Mae's past while Jessica and Kim shared college classes at Texas Tech. From World War II and forward, Ms. Eunice had been on quest after quest, which had proven to be no small part of the barrier that stood between Eunice Mae and her Southern-bred, high-minded relatives from Savannah, Georgia.

Jessica's imagination ran wild as she considered all of the possibilities. She pictured her name beneath an in-depth, descriptive article, complete with *her* photos, featuring Eunice Mae Howell and her colorful life.

The next thing she knew, they had arrived in Ms. Eunice's driveway. There Matt stood, with the door wide open, staring at her.

"Oh. Sorry. My mind drifted off a little."

"I'll say," said Matt. "You have been uncharacteristically quiet since we left Ransom Canyon."

"Sorry. I didn't mean to be rude."

"Nonsense," said Eunice Mae. "I could hear the wheels turning all the way back here. It's a good sign—an active mind."

Matt waited for Jessica to step out of the car then pulled the seat back for Eunice Mae. Eunice Mae stood on tiptoe to whisper in Matt's ear. He leaned down to meet her.

"She's a keeper, Matthew. Take care how you treat this one."

Eunice Mae had some sort of insight Matthew chose not to argue with. He could not see where he and Jessica might go from here, anyway, so decided it might be best to keep his under-developed opinion to himself.

"Yes, ma'am."

Matt escorted Eunice Mae to her front door, accepted the offered peck on the cheek then turned back toward the car. Taken unawares, he stared at the sight before him.

Jessica had lowered the top on the convertible and sat sideways in the seat, smiling at him. An open smile that drew him to her with the power of an emotion he had not formerly known. Her magnetic eyes shone in the light of the moon, and her straight, white teeth enhanced her beauty all the more.

This one could be trouble. No matter what Ms. Eunice might think.

But he didn't stop walking toward her. Didn't think he could stop what might come next, even if he tried. And at the moment, he had no desire to try. None whatsoever.

Chapter 5

How abundant are the good things that you have stored up for those who fear you, that you bestow in the sight of all, on those who take refuge in you

(Psalm 31:19 NIV).

JESSICA woke the following morning with a burning desire to act on her idea to exalt the life of Eunice Mae Howell. She showered and dressed quickly. Breakfast consisted of cinnamon raisin Ezekiel bread, toasted and spread with organic almond butter, and an apple. She grabbed a bottle of Real Water (her latest discovery) on her way out the door, and made a beeline for Eunice Mae's house.

The drive to Eunice Mae Howell's house took Jessica up Quaker Avenue, under Loop 289, and across town to 19th Street. This would be Jessica's first visit to Eunice Mae's famous home. It stood out from the other forms of architecture on that wide, beautiful street that served as the geographic location of many, high-end, unique estates.

Eunice Mae's home had been featured in *Texas Monthly* the month following its complete transport and resurrection. Jessica's mom had saved that particular edition, and had been so awed by the story, that the magazine still graced the coffee table in the den, protected by a heavy duty cover designed for that purpose.

Jessica's heart kicked up a notch when she pulled into the driveway of Eunice Mae's home. She paused for several minutes to take it all in. She smiled at the memory of what she'd read regarding its history.

The plantation homes depicted in movies paled in comparison to see the magnificent structure up close. A wide wrap-around porch supported by gleaming white columns seemed like open arms to any guests who might venture up the bloom-lined path that led to the four-foot wide front door.

Old and glorious magnolia trees which had been planted long in advance supported the southern theme, and added an inviting scent that blended with the fragrant shrubs and flowers that made up the balance of the landscape.

Jessica smiled, breathed in a long, cleansing breath, and made her way up the stone path to the porch then across to the front door. She stood on the doorstep with her camera slung over her shoulder and a backpack on her back. This self-appointed assignment had her more excited than any single assignment she'd had for a solid year. Her hope, not only to introduce Eunice Mae's character to the world, would be that a major magazine, like *Newsweek* or *Time*, or even *USA Today*, would take it and run with it, as a series. Jessica felt strongly that this amazing woman's contribution to society deserved a cover story.

Eunice Mae answered the door with a smile on her face—a face that belied her age. Her body had remained slim and fit; and she wore a pair of Not Your Daughter's Jeans with ease. She had slipped on a violet, polished-cotton shirt over a camisole that morning because she liked the feel of it against her skin. She wore her hair cut in a modern style, unwilling to succumb to blue hair and brush rollers.

Her face radiant, Eunice Mae opened the door wide so Jessica would feel welcome.

"Come in, Jessica. I'm so glad you could make it."

"Thank you. How are you this morning?"

"I woke up again, and I intend to enjoy every moment left to me."

"I admire you, Ms. Eunice. And I can hardly wait to hear about your life."

Eunice Mae laughed, closed the door behind Jessica then led her into the kitchen.

"Are you a coffee drinker?"

The smell of fresh-brewed coffee permeated the air.

"No, ma'am. But I have always loved the way it smells."

"I love the smell, too. But I've had a coffee habit for 70 years now, and don't intend to give it up," she said with a laugh. "Anyway, have a seat, dear. I'll join you at the bar soon as I doctor up the coffee enough to make it palatable."

Eunice laughed at the notion then turned away from Jessica, to prepare her coffee.

Jessica settled on the bar stool at the end of the long granite countertop and watched this elegant lady move with grace. Eunice Mae showed her heart to everyone. You didn't have to guess how she felt about you, or any subject that might come up, for that matter. Jessica smiled, and found herself wanting to grow up and be real, be brave, be unstoppable—just like Eunice Mae Howell.

Eunice Mae moved from the Keurig coffee maker to the refrigerator. Jessica's eyes got big as Eunice Mae pulled out a large tray of fresh fruit and dip, set it on the bar then turned back to retrieve a second tray of cheeses. Once the trays, two china plates, cloth napkins and heavy silver had been arranged around a vase filled with colorful Gerber daisies, Eunice Mae placed her mug of cream-laden coffee on the bar at the opposite end from Jessica. She smiled. A smile that lit up her face and eyes.

"Can't help it," said Eunice Mae. "My southern raisin' won't let me have a guest I don't at least attempt to feed."

"And I appreciate your hospitality. If we talk long enough, I'll take advantage of it."

And they did.

For the next five hours, Jessica and Eunice Mae visited. Ms. Eunice pulled out picture albums, and journals, and letters. They laughed and cried and shared their hearts. And Jessica snapped picture after picture. She took pictures of old photographs, and any journal entries that Eunice Mae would allow. Eunice Mae posed in the garden, in the living room, the den, and in the kitchen.

Jessica left with a full heart, a swimming head, and a good deal of material, as well as Eunice Mae's gracious permission to pitch her idea with zeal.

Matt glanced up as his mother came into the kitchen.

"Good morning, Mrs. Churchwell."

Catherine laughed. "I'm almost used to it."

"He's a good man, Mom. Really. I'm happy for you."

For a minute, Matt was tempted to tell his mother everything that filled his heart. His anxiety over the death of his father, an ache that refused to go away. About the talk he'd had with Tommy on the porch in Tennessee, all those many Thanksgivings ago. And about his concern for Kimberly and the turn her life might take because of poor choices. And most of all, he wanted to share his testimony, put her mind to rest, so she would know without a shadow of a doubt that Matthew Baldwin loved the Lord, had asked Him into his heart, and trusted Him with his eternal destination.

But he had a mission to fulfill this morning, and decided to put off the heavy stuff until a better time.

"Thanks," said Catherine. "He is a good man, and we both deserve to be happy. So, what's interesting in the newspaper?"

"Not much. Thought it was time I got a job."

"So, you'll be staying in the area?"

Matt grinned. His mother and Kim, his two greatest admirers, would be thrilled for him to settle down somewhere close. Close enough to visit on a regular basis. Close enough to make short-notice plans. Close enough to hug.

Thunder crashed and Catherine jumped.

"Sorry. The sound of thunder in August is always a surprise."

"A welcome one."

"Yes, sir. Very welcome. My water bill in July was ridiculous."

Matt went back to the original subject and answered his mother's question.

"I am considering staying in the area," said Matt. "Pretty much depends on the job market."

His mother remained silent.

"But I promise to try," he said.

"Good. And I promise to pray."

Matt and Catherine drank coffee and shared sections of the *Avalanche Journal* for another half hour.

"Well, I think I'll pound the pavement for a while and see what I can stir up. I'll see you later, Mom. Wanna have lunch?"

"Lunch would be lovely. Just the two of us, or should I call Tommy?"

"Tommy's always welcome."

Matt leaned down and planted a kiss on top of his mother's head. What a treasure of a mother. He should have told her many years ago, and many times. He made a mental note: *Learn to show your emotions. The people who have loved you, no matter what, deserve to know you love them too.*

"Text me when you and Tommy decide when and where," he said. "It's your town, so I'll let you pick. Just gonna run upstairs and change. I thought I'd take the car; don't want to be rejected on first impressions alone. And a Harley might not make the best one."

Catherine watched her son stroll away, with that swagger he'd carried since his early teens. What a scary kid he had been to raise. Didn't have a fearful bone in his body.

A chill raced up her back as a few of those close calls crashed through her brainwaves. Bicycle crashes. Motorcycle crashes. Fights on the playground while defending his older brothers, who had all developed smaller physiques. Disappearing on warm days, without telling a soul where he was going. Signing up for the Navy without one minute's discussion. The list was long and unnerving.

Thank You, Lord, for bringing him home to us, safe and whole, and apparently all grown up. Help him find a home for his restless spirit, and a godly woman to capture his heart.

Matt stood on Eunice Mae's doorstep, cap in hand. A beautiful, new, fitted cap he had picked up a short hour earlier at the airport. He ran his thumb over the embossed logo, waiting for Eunice Mae to answer the door.

At long last, the secret would be revealed. He'd had a hard time not spilling the beans to his mother at breakfast.

The door opened, interrupting his thoughts, and Matt found himself looking into the stunning blue-green eyes of Jessica Roberts.

"Hello."

"You look surprised to see me."

"I guess I am."

"Well, come on in. Ms. Eunice and I are just finishing up. I am given to understand that y'all are having lunch today."

"Yes, with Mother and Tommy at the Cattle Baron."

He paused for a moment as he followed Jessica into the den.

"Uh, you're welcome to join us," he said, as she turned to face him in the arched doorway. Her captivating eyes never failed to hold him in their grip. He would have to figure out what to do about that. Jessica Roberts had qualities he admired. Good qualities, wrapped in a tiny package of what? Dynamite? Nitroglycerine? Or just good old fashion appeal, loaded with adrenaline?

A frightening thought suddenly occurred to him. He would have to ask himself how he felt about moving 350 miles away from her. And wondered if it would matter much to her, when he did.

"Thanks. But I have a deadline to meet," he heard her say, bringing him back to the moment.

Only a few seconds had passed, but it seemed much longer. He had to shift back into "normal" mode and converse with her on a level befitting the circumstances. Anything deeper would have to wait for another day.

"What are you working on? I'd like to read it," he managed to say, his heart hidden beneath a straight face and neutral expression. It had to be a good idea to show interest in what interested her, right? And it wasn't a phony question. He really did have an interest in what interested Jessica.

His question remained unanswered when Eunice Mae spotted him in the entryway.

"Good morning, Matthew," she said. "Come in and have a seat. We still have a few minutes before we need to leave."

"Well, I don't," said Jessica. "I gotta scoot."

Jessica crossed the room to Eunice Mae's chair, gave her a peck on the cheek, and said, "Thanks again for your time. It's been quite an eye-opener. I can hardly wait to see the photos on glossy paper and your story in print. You are totally amazing."

"Thank you, dear. Life has been quite invigorating for me. Run along now. I know you're in a hurry. And congratulations on nailing the assignment. I was very impressed that they accepted your submission."

"Major crazy, and way cool. Well, I'll see you soon, Ms. Eunice. I really gotta go."

"Of course, dear."

"I'll call you," said Matt.

Jessica smiled her killer smile, and said, "I'd like that."

Yes, Matt wondered how he would manage with 350 miles of interstate stretched between himself and Jessica Roberts.

Chapter 6

You make known to me the path of life; you will fill me with joy in your presence, with eternal pleasures at your right hand (Psalm 16: 11 NIV).

JESSICA hurried out to her car, grinning big. Not only had *Time* magazine accepted her proposal and agreed to run five full-length articles, complete with full-page, full-color photos, covering the life of Ms. Eunice Mae Howell, but Matthew Baldwin had said he'd call her. She honestly did not know which prospect thrilled her the most.

She hugged the leather portfolio to her chest and twirled in a circle.

"It's a great day to be alive."

In her euphoria, Jessica had forgotten all about her commitment to the *Avalanche Journal*, and grimaced when the phone cried, "I owe my soul to the company store," the ringtone she had assigned to the Editor in Chief.

"Hello. Yes, sir. I'm headed your way now."

A staff meeting had been scheduled for 11:00 AM. It was now 11:15. She'd been in a hurry to meet the first deadline requirement for *Time*, which made it easy for a dull thing like a staff meeting to fly right out of her memory banks.

Catherine and Tommy parked in front of the Cattle Baron at 82nd and Quaker, next to the vehicle that had become Matt's personal calling card. Catherine smiled every time she saw it. So many good memories filled her heart, memories of her father and the dozens of times he had strapped her in the back seat and drove around the block with the top down.

"My dad loved that car," she said, as she joined Tommy on the sidewalk.

"Yeah. I've heard a few stories, especially about the hours and hours he spent keeping it showroom-floor pristine."

"Drove my mother crazy sometimes," said Catherine with a laugh. "He would be so proud that Matthew shares his passion."

"Speaking of Matthew," said Tommy, taking a step toward the restaurant entrance.

"I'm ready," said Catherine. She traced her finger around the Cadillac emblem on the hood then turned to go. "I still miss him, you know."

"Yes, I do," said Tommy. "Loss is hard for all of us."

When they entered the restaurant, they were led to the table where Matt and Eunice Mae waited for them. Matt stood while his mother took the seat Tommy pulled out for her.

"Hello everyone," said Catherine.

The usual greetings were exchanged, and a waiter came around to take their orders.

"So, do you have news, Ms. Eunice?" said Catherine.

"Well, Jessica does. She submitted her idea to run a series about my crazy life, and *Time* magazine jumped on it."

"That's super," said Catherine.

"Congratulations, Ms. Eunice," said Tommy.

"That calls for a toast," said Matt.

They had been served water upon their arrival, so they each raised a glass toward Eunice Mae.

"To the most famous WASP in Lubbock County," said Matthew.

"Here, here," chimed Tommy and Catherine, in unison.

No one could argue with that.

"Thank you. Thank you," said Eunice Mae, nodding her head in gracious acceptance of their sincere flattery. "I'll take a bow later. But that's enough about me. I think it's time Matthew shared his big news."

She cut her eyes toward him, raised her glass a second time, and said, "Go ahead, dear. They deserve to know."

Catherine stared at him. What could Eunice Mae possibly mean? Catherine tried to think what might be coming. Deserved to know?

What did they deserve to know? The phrase conjured up strange feelings. And what would Matthew have told Eunice Mae that he hadn't told her? She stopped herself from thinking about it. He may have excellent news, and her speculation could ruin everything. So, keeping a neutral expression, Catherine braced herself for whatever Matt had to tell them.

"Do you want the good news or the bad news first?"

Bad news? Oh dear. Catherine's mind tried to push her toward the dark side again. But she refused to listen to the tug at her heart. Maybe it wouldn't be *that* bad.

"Never end with bad news, Matthew," Catherine heard Eunice Mae say. "It disturbs the pallet, and leaves a bad taste."

"Yes, ma'am, Ms. Eunice. So, anyway, the bad news is I'll be moving to Dallas at the end of next month."

"Oh," said Catherine, with a little hiccup. "Well, that's not so bad."

Catherine inhaled a deep breath of relief. If Dallas was the bad news, she could relax. Dallas really wasn't so bad, was it?

"We can live with Dallas," she continued. "At least you'll be in Texas. What's taking you there?"

Matt pulled the fitted cap out of his back pocket then down over his hair.

Catherine gasped. "Oh, my word; you're going to be a commercial pilot."

Elation quickly replaced the anxiety that had begun to build. A commercial pilot. Wonderful.

"Congratulations, Matt," said Tommy. "Those jobs are not easy to come by."

"No, sir. And I wouldn't have the job now, if not for Ms. Eunice."

"Oh, p-shaw," said Eunice Mae. "Even with my connections, we had to wait over a year for an opening."

Over a year, thought Catherine. Matthew had been keeping a secret for nearly two years. Apparently, Kim didn't even know this one. Over a year. That's a long time to wait for a job opening. Thinking about it, she could understand Matt's secrecy. What if things hadn't turned out like he'd hoped? No, he had done the right thing by waiting to tell them until he had a confirmed offer. And of course, he had told Eunice Mae. She had been working behind the scenes to help make this happen. Matt could have ended up anywhere; but God had smiled on them and held an opening for her son in his home state.

Thank You, Lord. It would have been extremely difficult to watch him fly far away from home again. Thank You. Thank You so much.

Catherine reined in her thoughts and tried to focus on what Eunice Mae was saying.

"Knowing he did not plan to re-enlist, Matthew applied while still on active duty," Eunice Mae was saying. "And besides, if your record didn't speak for itself, Matthew, they wouldn't have hired you, no matter what anyone said."

"I like the way Southwest does business," said Tommy. "And they have a superb safety record."

"Being a pilot comes with some perks, for sure," said Matt. "The first few years I'll get the least desirable schedule, of course, so I may have to be creative with Christmas and Thanksgiving. But over all I'm very pleased with the package. And family flies free, if you don't mind standby."

Matt had signed his name on the bottom line. Now he had six weeks to find a place to live and relocate. Shouldn't be too difficult. It's not like he'd never moved before. He'd been lots of places with the Navy, been in live-fire combat situations, and walked away without a scratch. So, why did he have an uneasy feeling about moving now? He would be based in a great city, be able to make new friends, and fly in a whole new way. And his family could fly for free. But something still niggled at him.

He leaned back in the lounge chair and began to pray. Had he done the right thing? At the time he'd applied, he had been very sure. But that was years ago. Before he'd come home, spent time with his family. Before he'd met Jessica Roberts.

Here he sat, just hours after the deal had been made and he couldn't find peace. So, he picked up the Bible from the end table and began to read. Psalm 32, verse eight of the NIV translation: *The Lord says, "I will make you wise and show you where to go. I will guide you and watch over you."*

Couldn't be more spot-on than that. Matt settled back into the chair to read more. He had learned, during his early years in the Navy, that he could trust God's word far more than the thoughts in his own head, or the opinions of any man.

His flight instructor back then had been a strong and courageous man of God. Even as Matt read the Bible, many of the life lessons he'd learned from Lieutenant Colonel Masterson came to mind. Each of those lessons had served Matt well, both in and out of the cockpit.

As he sat there, absorbing God's love letter to His children, he remembered other men who had been available at the very moment he needed guidance, or a diversion from temptation. And the Lord reminded him that during all the years he'd been gone, Maggie, Tommy, his mother, grandmother, and siblings had prayed for him.

"Thank You, Lord," whispered Matt.

Humbled and blessed, Matt closed his eyes and let the love of God surround him. He rested in peace as Holy Spirit comforted and encouraged him. After a time, Matt opened his eyes and re-read Proverbs 16:3. "Lord God, according to Your word, if I wholeheartedly commit whatever I do to You, my plans will succeed."

Matt smiled as he gently closed the Bible, convinced that Dallas was indeed where he needed to be. Now he just had to figure out how to tell Jessica. And then figure out what life might be like, without her.

Jessica ran down the hall to the editor's office. She slipped inside and took the first empty seat.

Mr. Morrison frowned when he noticed her.

"Glad you could join us," he said, his voice laced with sarcasm.

"Sorry."

The meeting picked up where the editor had left off. Jessica felt certain she'd not heard the last about being a half hour late for a staff meeting. But she would worry about that when the time came. Right now, she would pay attention. She did still have a job to do. And she intended to do it well, for as long as it lasted.

Even so, the assignment she had acquired with *Time* magazine would take a lot of the sting out of whatever Mr. Morrison might have to say.

One week after his job acceptance, Matt made good on his promise to call Jessica. It had not been a difficult decision. He had liked Jessica from the moment they'd met. And nothing had happened to change his mind. She fascinated him. Independent and feisty, beautiful, and genuinely interesting. She had worked to move up in the ranks as a photo journalist. And he loved the fact that Jessica admired Ms. Eunice. As an adopted member of their family, it seemed important that the two of them get along.

And then there was the fact that Jessica didn't hang all over him, or call him every hour. Point in fact, she hadn't called him at all. Also an important factor in what he considered to be a healthy relationship. Jessica worked hard, and worked out—definitely fascinating.

He waited for her to pick up, whistling as he paced the floor of the basement bedroom, where Maggie had lived. There were remnants of her still in the room. The mantle clock she had purchased with her own money, an allowance she had received from Catherine's parents, she'd said. At thirteen years of age, and abandoned by her biological family, she had bragged to Matthew many times that she was not an indentured servant, or a paid housekeeper. She was a family member, working for an allowance. She had saved for many months to buy the treasured timepiece. Matt had been struck by the fact that the house where Maggie had lived as a young child had not offered even one clock, on any wall or dresser, in any room. But Matt's own mother loved clocks so much, you could find a minimum of one clock in every room, even the bathrooms. The clock Maggie had left to Matt. Soon after her death, Matt had moved into Maggie's room. The room had a peace about it, an alluring quality that calmed Matt every time he entered the space. He didn't consider that she had died on the very bed he slept in; but it reminded him that she had passed into the heavenly portals from that very space. Made his heart glad that she had been transported to live forever with her Savior.

"Hello," he said, as Jessica answered and jerked him back to the moment. Alert and anxious to connect with her again, Matt said the first thing that came to mind. "How are you?"

The first thing most people would say. Even people who barely know one another. People who meet on the street, and might never meet again. And didn't really expect an answer. Matt hoped he didn't sound lame, because he really did care how things were with Jessica. Really.

Jessica gave him an update on her latest project, and how she had barely made the deadline. She was ready to pour all of herself into being an independent contractor; so the drudgery of everyday happenings left her antsy, at best.

"Are you too worn out to have dinner with me and maybe take in a movie?"

Matt ran his hand along the edge of the dresser as he paced, waiting. Why he would be nervous baffled him. He couldn't remember ever feeling this way. Ever. He was asking a girl to go out. Big deal. Except he was acting like he'd never done it before. He kept pacing, waiting.

Several seconds passed before Jessica answered; but she agreed to go out with him. It felt good, *wanting* to have a date. He'd spent so many years avoiding the kind of women he seemed inevitably to attract, Jessica had been a breath of fresh air. A wild rose in a field of ordinary daisies. Getting to know her could be interesting. Fun even.

He suddenly realized he hadn't used the word "fun" in years. He'd had adventures, plenty of them, and a lot of excitement over the years, but not much fun. He'd been serious about his vocation, serious about his duty to the Navy, and reckless with his personal life. Maybe Jessica could help change that. He'd just have to wait and see.

Matt glanced at his watch—eight hours before date time. What should he do with himself? Today wasn't a significant Friday. His mother had left the house early that morning, and he had no idea how long she would be gone. He thought a moment. Maybe he would go through his boxes and see what needed to be stored, and what he might be able to use.

Matt hadn't kept a lot of memorabilia from the service. His pea coat, his dog tags, a stack of letters from his mother and little Kim. Kim wasn't so little anymore, but he still thought of her that way. His favorite sibling. She had loved him unconditionally, innocently. Had trusted him completely. His first full-on, no-holds-barred admirer. She had become a fine lady. An inspiration, really. Apparently, she had made peace with the past, after being the only child who had not known their father, or played in their house, or swam in their pool, or run foot races up and down the curved stairwell that led to their father's study. She had come to Texas alone, unsure of what she would find here, afraid of their grandmother, whom Kim had never met.

She came, and she faced it all alone. The house, the journals, the people, the university. A child in search of herself, in search of some tangible evidence that her father had loved her, even before she'd been born. Had loved them all. But still, something seemed unsettled deep within Kim's soul. From what he'd heard, relationships didn't seem to work out for Kim, an issue he would check into with her, as soon as she slowed down enough to have a serious conversation. Even so, Kim had assured him that she had found a measure of peace in this house, in regard to their father.

Perhaps now, it would be his turn.

A tear slipped down his face, and he closed up the box he'd been rummaging through. He placed it on top of the other boxes in the closet and left the room. His mind had wandered to the topic of Kim and their dad; and he no longer cared about the boxes.

He took the stairs up to the kitchen, made himself a turkey and cheese on rye, and poured a glass of milk. He sat down at the table in the breakfast nook and finished off the small meal. He then wandered across the living room to the entrance of his mother's bedroom. He stepped inside the doorway. To his left still stood the lifelike portrait of his mother and most of her children. Kim had not made that pose, it being made the year before her birth. The painting made a striking impression. Catherine, with her long French braid across one shoulder, sat poised and erect, serenity giving her eyes a special glow. All five of them were dressed in white, with perfect hair and tranquil expressions. The painting rested in a large oval frame, depicting lifelike, life-sized members of the Baldwin family.

Matt stopped to stare at it for a moment. It seemed almost prophetic—a beautiful mother and her four children, but with an almost agonizing absence of a father. The picture had been there for so long, he hadn't paid much attention to it, till now. He thought back to the long, drawn-out ordeal of posing for it, and had to laugh. Of course, he'd been the restless one who had required an extra measure of stern looks from Maggie, to stay still for such a long, boring task.

He moved past the portrait and over to the stairway that led to his father's study. Kim had told him of her journey through their father's journals. She had left them where she'd found them.

As he reached the top of the landing, he froze. He could hardly believe what he was seeing. His father's study—exactly as he remembered it. He stood in the doorway for a moment, just staring. Behind him, the sun shone through vertical blinds, and fell across a stack of books on the desk, in front of the chair, still pulled out at an angle, as though his father had left to retrieve something—and never come back.

Matt stepped into the room. He ran a finger along the edge of the double-wide desk. He swiveled the chair, amazed that the squeak he remembered, still squeaked. He moved from there to the giant world globe, and gave it a slow spin. Spinning it with any iota of speed had never been allowed. He grinned at himself for automatically obeying this long-ago entrenched habit.

The shelves of books caught his attention, and Matt stepped forward. He approached the exact shelf Kim had told him contained their father's journals. The binding of each volume contained beginning to ending dates. He reached for the journal that showed entries from the year Matt had turned seven, the year before he'd lost his dad. His heart wasn't ready to read the sadness his dad's journal must necessarily contain from that year. The year his father must have been aware that his time was short. Matt settled into the comfy, familiar, distressed leather sofa. He flipped through the journal to an earlier time, and read his father's words:

March 3 – I have three fine sons. Paul, our first-born, James, and Matthew. I feel led to pray a special prayer for each one of them. Paul, who shows early signs that we named him in accordance with the leadership of the Holy Spirit. At this tender age, he is already passionate about the Lord. Every week, we take one of his classmates to church with us. I pray, Lord, that You protect his heart, teach him to trust in You, no matter what. Guide him along the narrow path, and grow his faith as he seeks Your face.

And James, already mature in technological advancements, has a keen mind for detail, an understanding of the way things work. The spiritual gift test we gave him suggests a career in computers. He'll be a tremendous asset to whatever company he joins, or whatever community he becomes a part of. God has a special way of making all things work together for good, for those who love Him and are called according to His purpose. And He keeps His promises. He has promised to bless those who love Him—to a thousand generations.

And what can I say about Matt? He is still so young…

Matt sat up taller against the back of the couch, eager to find out how his father truly felt about him. Had he loved him the way Matt had believed he did? Had he approved of him? Would he read praise or concern in his father's own hand? Matt returned to the journal entry with a fresh enthusiasm.

> *...and already a heartthrob for every girl in his class. He is too young to appreciate the finer points of the female persuasion, but I have no doubt, he will catch on at the proper time. I love the way his face lights up when I come into a room. I love that he is enthusiastic about an hour of playing catch in the back yard, or how thoroughly he took to swimming after just one lesson, or that he already wears me out on the basketball court. He loves so many things, and his penchant for remembering the make and model of every car on the road is nothing short of remarkable. A real man's man, built for adventure, Matt seems to have no fear...*

Matt pulled his eyes from the page and stared across the room. No fear. That was true, for a while. For the next year, anyway. Until his father died. Fear set in the moment they pulled out of the driveway and left behind the only home he had ever known. He had battled the fear in unconventional ways. He made sure nothing would scare him again. He pushed himself to be the best at everything. He stood up to bullies. He joined the service to fight the enemy—and made sure he came back alive. As though he could control such things. He had run from close relationships. Run from romance. Run from love. Run from potential heartbreak.

Matt relaxed and closed his eyes. A tiny ray of light passed through a crack in the thick wall that had surrounded his heart since the death of his dad. He knew now, his father had loved him, had noticed him, had believed in him. He had read the words in his father's own hand.

"Matt, are you in the house?"

The sound of his mother's voice brought him back to reality. To present day. He had instantly been transported from an imaginary game of baseball with his dad, to being a grown man with much to be grateful for.

"Up here, Mom! I'll be right down!"

Matt set his father's journal gingerly on the low coffee table in front of the familiar leather couch.

"Thanks, Dad," he said, as he turned to go. "I loved you, too."

Matt scurried down the spiral staircase, feeling lighter than he had in years. His father had loved him, had believed in him. It seemed like he had crossed an invisible barrier. Had stepped out of the darkness and into the light. He felt good. Really good.

He came up short just inside the great room.

"Oh. Hello, Jess."

"Are you in the middle of something? I can come back another time."

The look in her eyes, as much an apology as an invitation, took his breath away.

"No, I was just." What he felt at the moment could easily overshadow anything Jessica might have to say. She looked so distraught, he decided to save his good news for another day. "Well, it doesn't matter," he said. "What can I do for you?"

"Take me for ice cream?"

"Ice cream," he repeated.

"If you're not busy."

Matt looked toward his mother, who was grinning from ear to ear.

"Okay," he said slowly. "Ice cream sounds good. Doesn't matter to me if we start our date a little early."

Strange. Why would Jessica show up here a few hours before their date was scheduled to start? Maybe she just got anxious to see him. But that's not how he interpreted the expression in her eyes. Something must be on her mind that couldn't wait. He had meant what he'd said. It didn't matter how soon their date started; he would just get to spend more time with her. The moment felt awkward, though. Should he try to include his mother? She was standing right there.

"Uh, would you care to join us, Mother?"

"Heavens no," said Catherine, with a laugh. "I've been slacking on rehearsal time this month, and I have a concert in North Carolina next Friday night. Maybe next time."

Maybe next time, thought Matt. *I know what you're doing. You're conspiring with Ms. Eunice in a game of match-making.*

He grinned at his mother and bowed in Jessica's direction.

"My car or yours, Madam?"

"Oh. It will have to be yours," said Catherine. "I picked Jessica up and brought her over."

"That's odd," said Matt.

"Not really," said Jessica. "I asked her if she would."

"So, a conspiracy, is it?"

"Maybe," said Jessica. "I was in the mood for ice cream, and hoped you would be too. I didn't want to wait till tonight."

Matt didn't know what to say to that, so he just shrugged his shoulders, gave her a wink, and offered his hand. She took it, and they went out through the kitchen to the four-car garage out back.

"I'll be home relatively early, Mom."

"Have a good time, you two."

Chapter 7

And everyone who calls on the name of the Lord will be saved
(Acts 2:21 NIV).

JESSICA settled into the passenger seat of Matt's Cadi and breathed a sigh of relief. At least Matt had not laughed in her face and refused to see her. In reality, she could have waited till evening, but couldn't bear the strain any longer; thus, had taken it upon herself to ask for Catherine's help.

Matt had been on her mind for days, so when he called and asked her out, the longing to talk with him got pushed into high gear. She didn't know if he might feel anything close to what she felt for him, but she wanted to find out if they had any chance at all. For something. Sometime in the foreseeable future. But she knew nothing substantial could happen until the question burning in her heart got settled.

She watched him through the side-view mirror then through the rear-view mirror as he made his way to the driver's side door. Soon as he settled behind the wheel, however, she averted her eyes and stared straight ahead.

After a moment, before he started the car, he turned to face her.

"Wanna tell me what's going on? I haven't known you very long, but you don't much seem like the chase-a-man type."

She didn't smile as he raised an eyebrow and made no move to insert the key into the ignition.

"Well?" he said.

It took a minute for Jessica to find her voice.

"I was hoping you wouldn't be quite so intuitive," she said. "I thought we could just go for ice cream, and pretend it's a lovely day."

"We can, if that's what you really want."

"Let's start out that way, if you don't mind. I'd like to give my brain a break. It's been way over-thinking everything lately."

"That, I can live with."

Matt raised the garage door, started the engine then backed into the alley. Arrowhead Drive sported super-clean, well-groomed, landscaped alleyways. As they rolled to the corner, Jessica kept her head turned and her eyes on the beautiful Elizabeth Taylor pink rose bushes that lined the back fence of 106 Arrowhead Drive. The address had a history that had kept tongues wagging all over Lubbock County for decades. Jessica had been knee-deep in the drama as a college student, had watched the miraculous re-joining of a family long-ago split apart. She had witnessed the almost unbelievable transformation of Matt's infamous grandmother, Elizabeth Baldwin, who had been a tyrant—unforgiving, manipulative, cruel and heartless—before Jesus changed her heart.

Jessica had observed Elizabeth Baldwin from a distance, secretly, without sharing her doubts with Elizabeth's granddaughter—and Jessica's best friend—Kimberly Baldwin. She hadn't dared do anything to jeopardize their relationship. Kim meant too much to her, then and now. When the truth came out about Kim's grandmother, Jessica had stood beside Kim, and helped her in every way she could. She'd had no idea she would one day be sitting in a car with Kim's big brother, with her heart tied in knots. Matt Baldwin appeared to be the type of man any girl with a brain would go to great lengths to marry. She felt silly. Their relationship could not yet be defined as a relationship; more of an acquaintance; so how had marriage found its way into her head?

Jessica released a sigh, as though she were alone in her apartment, and not in the car with Kim's favorite brother.

"You okay?" she heard Matt say, his voice penetrating her musings.

Jessica jumped in spite of herself.

"Jessica," said Matt. "I'm not going to bite you. What's making you so jumpy?"

"Could we get that cone at Sonic?" she said, not really answering the question. "I want to talk to you, to try and explain myself—but not in a public forum. Please," she said, unable to make herself smile, or use any charming, beguiling sentiment. Her heart was afraid. Afraid to reveal itself, afraid someone would know she didn't measure up to what other people thought of her. People she cared deeply about. She wanted, desperately, to be honest with someone who would not judge her too harshly. She hoped and prayed she could trust Matt with her secret.

The pleading look Jessica gave him seemed so out of character, Matt hesitated to answer—but only for a moment. He knew that <u>he</u> couldn't be the problem. They barely knew one another. So, why wasn't she approaching Kim with her troubles? Why pick him? He considered himself to be the least likely candidate for serving as a counselor. For anybody. His preacher brother would make more sense.

But when tears welled up in Jessica's eyes, Matt knew he would try his best to help her. He knew, even if he didn't have the answers she needed to hear, he would help her find someone who did.

Matt ordered two cones and two Route 44 Dr. Peppers before he turned the fan down on the air conditioner and angled in his seat to face Jessica. They would have a bit of a wait, it being happy hour, and not a single empty parking space.

"Okay, my friend. What is up with you?"

"I have a secret," said Jessica, "and I don't know who I should trust with it."

"So you picked someone you barely know?"

"I'm not sure yet. I know Kim trusts you. Can I?"

"I'd like to think so."

Jessica paused for so long, the car hop zoomed up to the window on roller blades before Jessica had disclosed the tiniest part of her secret.

Matt paid for their order, included a generous tip, then pulled his right knee up into the seat, and faced Jessica. He licked his ice cream in silence, more than mildly curious about the lady across the car from him.

Jessica finished every bite of the refreshing ice cream cone, wiped her mouth, and consumed a big gulp of Dr. Pepper before she had mustered the courage to broach the subject of her discomfort.

"I've decided," she said. "Maybe I can trust you, at that."

She smiled as Matt raised his right eyebrow again, as he was want to do. She had noticed the gesture several times. No words, just that raised brow. But anyone who knew him at all, understood the words that the look conveyed. A twinkle accompanied by humor. A burning, if troubled, countenance. A calmness, followed by concern and support. Jessica wondered if he had ever seen these tendencies in himself.

"Okay, I'll tell you," she said at last, suddenly unafraid. A knowing deep in her spirit confirmed that she could, indeed, trust Matthew Bradley Baldwin, with her deepest secret.

"But first, may I ask you a personal question?"

"Depends."

Jessica asked him straight out, not waiting to see if the question she had in mind would qualify as one he would be willing to answer.

"Have you accepted Jesus Christ as your personal Savior?"

The question surprised him. Was Jessica asking because she doubted that he had accepted God's free gift of grace? Could it be that she didn't have a relationship with Christ, herself? How vulnerable might she be, or sensitive, or defensive?

Matt sent up a prayer—a quick, desperate prayer for the right words. Words of grace and truth. He didn't want to mess up what had started to blossom between them. But he cared first and foremost for the eternal destiny of her soul than whether they became an item, or they didn't.

"I certainly don't mind answering that one," he said. "Yes, I have asked Jesus into my heart, to be my Lord and Savior."

"Why?" asked Jessica.

Matt heard no condescension or malice in her tone, so he decided to answer honestly, and share his testimony.

"Well, I was a late-bloomer, as Maggie would say. I remember being pretty mad at God when my father died. I had been in church my whole life. God had been portrayed as a loving God, who only wanted the best for His people. I got a little upset. I couldn't believe Dad's death could be good, in any way, shape, form, or fashion. I was an angry child, withdrawn and touchy at the same time. I finished fights, and started fights. I excelled in sports because my anger exploded on the football field, or basketball court, or baseball diamond, or track field.

"I was an angry teen and young adult. Right out of high school, I worked off-shore drilling to be away from people. People who cared about me. I alienated myself from my family, except for Kim, and a few postcards to Mother. I couldn't help but love Kim—she loved me so much. Blindly loved me. I joined the Navy so I would be far, far away from real life.

"Then I met a commanding officer who did not have an explosive temper. He didn't talk like other men I'd met in the Navy. He had a sense of humor, and endless patience.

"He sought me out one day, and straight-out asked me why I was so angry. I told him my story. For some reason I trusted him. He listened. He cared. He understood. His own father had passed away soon after the Captain's seventh birthday. My father died when I was eight. My commanding officer had survived many of the same struggles I faced. A youth pastor had led him to a saving knowledge of Jesus Christ then helped him embrace the love of God. The pastor tried to help him understand God's infinite wisdom. My commanding officer said it became his sworn duty to help everyone God put in his path, to lead them to the throne of grace. He said it was the least he could do, after what Christ had suffered for him.

"The decision to surrender to Christ changed my life, Jess."

Matt had not taken his eyes off Jessica, had not stopped praying.

"Did I answer your question?" he said at last. "Anything else you need to ask?"

Tears spilled over onto Jessica's cheeks, and Matt held his breath.

"I have another question," she said, between sniffles. "Will you help me receive the free gift too?"

Matt didn't say so, but he was amazed that Jessica had not crossed that bridge years ago.

Thank You for trusting me with this opportunity, Lord.

"I'd be honored. You can repeat after me or use your own words," he explained. "Before we begin, would you hand me the Bible that's in the glovebox?"

Matt reached across the seat to accept the chocolate brown, creased leather book, which had been a gift from his commanding officer.

"Mind reading a few verses? I'm pretty sure you've heard it all before; but when you're seeking salvation, the words seem to come alive when you speak them out loud."

Matt led Jessica through Romans 1:20 and 21; Romans 3:23; Romans 5:8; Romans 6:23; Romans 10:9 and 10; Romans 10:13; and Romans 11:36. His commanding officer had called these passages, collectively, the Roman Road. The Roman Road to salvation.

Jessica held the sacred book open in her lap, to the scripture reference Matt had encouraged her to read. Her hands trembled. Her voice sounded hollow and fearful at first. She spoke in a whisper. But as Matt fed the next scripture address to her, Jessica began to feel good about what she was reading. The words soothed her jangled nerves, and she began to believe God really did love her, that He wasn't angry that she had been slow to come around, slow to be willing to accept the love, grace, and mercy He had died to offer her. Slow to forgive Him for leaving her without a father.

By the time she had read Romans 10:13, Jessica almost shouted.

"Everyone who calls on the name of the Lord will be saved."

She looked at Matt, eyes brimming with tears. "Tell me what to say, Matt. I want this relationship sealed and solid."

"Yes, ma'am."

Matt repeated the simple words he had prayed when he experienced salvation for himself. Jessica listened, said the same words over again, in a whisper, a whisper of awe. She could feel herself changing. Feel her spirit swell, full of grace and truth. As "Amen and Amen" resounded through the vehicle, she refrained from shouting, but could not hold back the flood of tears that displayed a new level of joy she had yet to experience.

"You okay, Jess?"

"Better than I ever imagined I could be."

Jessica beamed with joy. The burden of not being loved by an earthly father had melted and slipped off her shoulders. Just like that. A miracle, and no small one. Like there could be a "small" miracle, anyway. A greater Father than she could ever dream up had <u>died</u> for her. Had made a way for love to change her life, her destiny, her eternity.

"Makes me very happy," said Matt.

"What do I do now?"

"The Bible says to make it public and be baptized—a Christian's first act of obedience."

Baptism. She knew about that. Had witnessed it numerous times through the years. She knew what to expect, and what it would mean. The entire church body would witness her public acceptance of Jesus Christ as her Savior. Once upon a time, that would have disturbed her. But today, she welcomed the opportunity.

"I can do that," she said. "Wait till my mother hears. She's been after me for years. I just always thought, since my dad left while I was a mere toddler, something must be bad wrong with me. We never heard from him again.

"Mother tried to tell me about God's love, and I let her, but I didn't listen, and I never tried to find out the truth for myself by digging into God's Word. Strange, how God sent a handsome man to help me realize His love is real. I'm glad, too, before I messed up and hurt your feelings."

"What do you mean?"

"You know, break up first, before anyone gets hurt. I've done it over and over. Avoidance seemed the safer path."

"I had that attitude myself once," said Matt. "God helped me see how self-centered and egotistical I was being. And now, He has sent a girl my way that I really want to get to know—and would rather not ever hurt—or avoid."

Jessica found herself looking forward to what God had planned for her. Maybe a real relationship with a real man who loved a real God. But she could wait. For now, being in love with Jesus felt really good. She asked Matt if he would take her to a book store and help her pick out a Bible of her own.

"Nothing I'd rather do more. It'll be more fun than a stuffy old dinner date. We can do that any time."

"I agree. And thanks for encouraging me, and sharing your heart with me."

"My pleasure. You can drop by for ice cream any time."

Chapter 8

For he guards the course of the just and protects the way of his faithful one
(Proverbs 2:8 NIV).

SOON after Jessica's conversion, Matt moved to Dallas. She had to admit, he had been open and honest with her. What she felt for him went much deeper than gratitude. She had fallen for him in a big way. She couldn't be sure if he'd been hit as hard as she had, but his tearful farewell had seemed genuine. Maybe he did care for her. Maybe they did have a future together. Some day. But right now, she intended to bloom where God had planted her. She was on a mission, and would have to deal with day-to-day demands, just like anyone else. Even so, she had placed Matthew Baldwin in a safe corner of her heart, and would deal with those emotions later.

"We'll find a way to get together," he'd said. "I'll call you."

Jessica shook off the fear and uncertainty, and pressed the doorbell at Eunice Mae Howell's home. Ms. Eunice could always be counted on to lift her spirits. And Jessica had a surprise for her.

When Eunice Mae opened the front door, Jessica heard her squeal then peeked over the top of the shiny new *Time* magazine.

"What do you think?" said Jessica.

"I think you're amazing," said Eunice Mae. "Come on in. We'll read it together."

On the fifteenth day of October, Matt found himself standing at a news stand in Dallas, Texas, and paying for all ten *Time* magazines the gentleman had on hand. Eunice Mae Howell smiled back at him from the cover, in her WASP uniform. A young, vivacious, brave, daring pilot, who served her country with pride, and without prejudice.

Matt loved Eunice Mae; but the name at the bottom right of the cover made his heart skip a beat. Jessica Roberts, photo journalist. He thought about her for a moment; but then decided to step out of line and take his thoughts to the coffee shop, where he could relax and read the entire article without interruption.

Article One—Young Eunice Mae Howell

Eunice Mae Howell, of Savannah, Georgia, graduated high school a year ahead of her class, at the tender age of 15, and immediately answered the compelling campaign to aid the war effort, and go to work.

She pushed up the sleeves of her newly acquired chambray shirt and defied her Southern-belle of a mother, whom she had driven to distraction with her notion to do her part, to make a difference.

"I'm going, Mother," said Eunice Mae. "I'm sorry you can't understand why, and won't accept the fact, but I am going. If you refuse to let me become a pilot, you could at least extend the courtesy of allowing me to rivet. We are, after all, at war. I can help; and help I shall."

Eunice Mae had taken 100% to the idea of becoming her own version of Rosie the Riveter. The campaign that flooded the U.S. with pleas for women to come to the aid of the men in uniform by joining the work force set her unconventional blood to boiling. Eunice Mae, much to her parents' dismay, had been born for more than frocks and frills. More than tea parties and piano recitals. Eunice Mae craved thrills. But more than that, patriotism had been birthed in her heart and grown with every news report she heard on the radio and every newspaper article she read.

Eunice Mae's responsibility as a riveter would take her far away from the family—to the ungodly state of Michigan (to hear her father say it), in some town he could not, and would not, pronounce properly. Ypsilanti.

"Ip-si-lan-tee, Daddy. Just call it Ipsee. People do that, or so I've heard. At least you would be acknowledging its existence."

"Ip. See," said Mr. Howell, slowly, deliberately, and with a load of sarcasm. "Satisfied?"

Eunice Mae shared a farewell dinner with her family then boarded a train the following morning. She arrived in Ypsilanti, Michigan on a snowy afternoon in mid-October, 1942. She checked into a boarding house with six other women, shared a meal with them, without sharing one thing about herself then collapsed onto a small, soft bed, in a room she shared with two other women.

Eunice Mae rose early and consumed the first available plate of eggs. The owner of the boarding house had a small farm where she raised chickens; and thus provided at least eggs in the morning and meat at night. Sometimes rice or potatoes, or greens, but always eggs and meat. Chicken meat. The ladies who lived in the boarding house had to be responsible for purchasing their individual portions of rationed goods. The cook seemed happy to prepare the simple fare, which made the exhausted boarders grateful for the time to shower before dinner and get to bed early.

Eunice Mae took her plate to the kitchen then made her way to the Willow Run Aircraft Factory, taking note of the route, and arrived before the doors opened. She waited outside as a light snow dotted her jacket, the warmest her mother had found in Savannah. Innocent, yet fiercely determined to be an asset to this factory that assembled B-24 bombers, Eunice Mae could have been mistaken as the poster model of Rosie the Riveter. She dressed in a similar shirt, sturdy pants and work boots, and had tied a bandanna around her hair. Her mother would not be pleased. But Eunice Mae Howell was determined to do her part in the war effort.

As the heavy door swung open, a large man with a stump for one leg stared down at her.

"What do you want?" he growled.

Eunice Mae, small in stature, but sturdy and courageous, stretched to her full height of five foot five inches. She pushed down any fear that might threaten to surface, and spoke clearly.

"A job. I am strong and capable, and want to do my part. Are you the person I need to talk to about hiring on?"

The big man laughed.

"A squirt like you?"

That wasn't the right thing to say to Eunice Mae Howell.

"You didn't answer the question," said Eunice Mae, moving a step closer. "Are you the foreman or aren't you?"

"No," he admitted. "But come on in, if you insist. I'll show you the way."

It took Eunice Mae Howell all of 30 days to make a name for herself in the factory. She stood up for the underdog who felt bullied by the supervisor. And once, she came between a white female riveter and a black female welder in order to bring about peace in the work place.

These women were using a whole new set of muscles, and an entirely different part of their brains—unfamiliar aches and pains accompanied hours of learning how to handle equipment, tools, and straw boss harassment from a bitter man—angry that the loss of half his right leg in a farming accident had kept him from fighting for his country.

Eunice Mae reported to work early and volunteered to stay late when they had a deadline to meet. She grew stronger and even more confident during the year she served at Willow Run. And every day, she fell more deeply in love with airplanes.

With her newly acquired confidence, Eunice Mae hopped a train, headed south at the close of her final day at the factory, bound and determined to serve as a pilot. Somebody had to fill the void. Men were needed for combat duty; and a few brave women had stepped forward to fill their shoes. This time, Eunice Mae did not ask her parents' permission, or even for their blessing, which she knew, full well, would not happen, in any case.

Eunice Mae arrived in Houston, Texas with a smile on her face and a secret in her luggage.

"My mother would have disowned me had she known it at the time," she explained to Nancy Love, the executive for all WASP ferrying operations. "I used my high school graduation money, which my parents felt certain I had secured in a bank vault, to take flying lessons."

"You didn't."

"The look on Nancy Love's face was priceless," Eunice Mae told me. "I recognized the same spark of determination and hunger for adventure that coursed through my blood."

We'll return now, to Eunice Mae's conversation with Nancy Love. I felt compelled to convey how deeply Ms. Eunice desired to serve her country. How seriously she took her role as a pilot.

"Oh, but I did," declared Eunice Mae. "I was found out later, of course. But for me, the summer after high school graduation will forever be glorious. I had convinced my very conservative parents that I needed some experience in the world of work. And I did work. That part wasn't a lie. I just didn't fully disclose that my clerical position happened to be in the hangar at a

private airfield. Anyway, I kept books, typed correspondence, scheduled flying assignments, and took flying lessons. I made my first solo flight at the end of July, and had tallied a total of a thousand flying hours before I left for Ypsilanti. How I managed to keep that secret, I'll never know."

This brave and determined young woman has done her country proud. Stay tuned for more adventures from the life of Eunice Mae Howell.

Matt flipped slowly back through the article, pausing to look at each picture, admiring his life-long friend as an adventurous young woman. What a corker, his grandpa would have said. Eunice Mae had done what Eunice Mae intended to do. As always.

As Matt mulled over Jessica's presentation of Eunice Mae Howell's life, it occurred to him how much he had been influenced by a long line of courageous, strong-willed, independent, yet loving and compassionate women.

Grandmother Baldwin, who had single-handedly just about destroyed the bonds of love in her own family. A miracle only God could orchestrate and carry out, had mended broken hearts and restored relationships. That same grandmother now used her administrative personality to organize fundraisers in support of unwed mothers and their babies, in honor of her own daughter who had experienced pregnancy outside of wedlock. Grandmother Baldwin, however, had been less fortunate in her physical health.

Although bound to a wheelchair due to crippling arthritis, her mind had remained sharp. In these latter years, she had done as much good as she had done harm in her earlier years. Her spiritual testimony alone had helped change the hearts of innumerable souls. Matthew had made peace with Grandmother Baldwin the day after he'd hired on with Southwest Airlines.

Grandmother Baldwin had called and invited him to the house. She, Matt, and Grandfather Baldwin sat in front of the expansive plate glass window that looked out over the vast Baldwin Estate. They shared a pitcher of sweet tea and a plate of Velda's homemade cookies.

Matt listened intently as his grandmother confessed her bitterness, anger, and frustration at the loss of her daughter, and how it had magnified in intensity at the loss of her son as well. She had been so angry, it had taken years of misery for her to even consider the possibility that God was indeed a God of love, who had her best interest in mind, and had a plan for her life. A plan that would give her hope and a future.

Matt had walked away from that meeting with a whole new perspective of the cruel and bitter woman Elizabeth Baldwin had been during his growing-up years. After all, her vindictive attitude had forced Mat's mother to leave their home at 106 Arrowhead Drive. His family had escaped her wrath, but had lived with only dark memories associated with her name. A name that had rarely been spoken in their Tennessee household. But when he'd overheard his mother talk about Elizabeth Baldwin the memories had not been pleasant.

As Matt closed the door behind him at Grandmother Baldwin's home, he thanked God for the miracle wrought within his grandmother's heart and life, while he'd been away, fighting for his country. For only a miracle could have reunited the Baldwin family, and grown them to be the close-knit family of today.

And Maggie. Dear, beloved Maggie. From Matt's earliest memories, her influence had been paramount. She had loved him, and scolded him. Had played catch with him, and forced him to complete his assignments for school. She had sat in silence while he lamented the restrictions placed upon him by rules and regulations. She had kept his secrets and prayed for him, out loud, so there would be no doubt that she cared about him, and believed God had a purpose for his life. It would have been nice to hear her voice again, to know she approved of him as a man, to share laughter and a plate of Mexican food with her, once again.

Then there was his mother. How brave she had been to walk away from the family home, uproot five children, and run for their lives. For many years he did not appreciate the depth of sacrifice and sorrow that had prompted the move. He hadn't understood it at the time, and didn't try to understand for a long, long time. He admired his mother now, though. Now that he knew the whole sad and frightening story. Getting to that point had taken some concentrated prayer, and a bucketful of forgiveness. The final piece of the puzzle had fallen into place when he read his father's journals. He had visited his father's study numerous times since that first one. He had laughed and cried, and laughed some more as he journeyed through the years, from his father's point of view.

The ringtone assigned to his mother interrupted Matt's musings. But he didn't mind, not now, since he had finished the article, and his cup of coffee, and good memories of her were fresh on his mind.

"Hi, Mom. What's up?"

"Well, I have a surprise for you. We are at the Anatole!"

"Really. And what brings you to town?"

"I'll be playing at Reunion Tower on Saturday night. What country will you be in?"

Matt smiled.

"I happen to be off this weekend. I filled in for a buddy last week, so we switched. I'm very excited you're here. I haven't seen you in action since I was a kid. I am invited, right?"

The sound of his mother's laughter tickled his ears; but his mind began to wonder what Jessica might be up to this weekend. A piano concert seemed a viable reason to invite her to Dallas.

Jessica Roberts, the girl who had captured his heart. He'd been in Dallas for six weeks and had only seen her once. That single memory kept her close to his heart—until he could see her again. He had sent her a round-trip ticket for a 3-day weekend, and it had taken no less than a miracle to come up with a date they could both utilize. He had put her up in the Anatole, treated her to a Stephan Pyles meal at

Southwestern Plaza, then to the latest show of Disney's Beauty and the Beast at Dallas Theater. Good clean fun between two good friends who had agreed to follow God's leading, and not spend time alone in a private setting during their courtship. It was old-fashioned and sneered at by some, but they respected each other and intended to do things God's way. It meant a lot to them to live clean and love clean, and trust the Lord with their future.

Jessica had seemed thrilled with all three segments of that date. Just hearing his mother say "Anatole" had taken Matt back to that amazing weekend.

"Are you available for dinner this evening?" said Catherine.

"I wish. It's Thursday, and my afternoon and evening today and tomorrow are packed. But can we get together before the show on Saturday?"

"Of course. You do whatever you need to do, and we'll see you downstairs in the lobby, say 3:00 Saturday afternoon?"

"Sounds great. Really glad you're here. Seems like I haven't seen anyone from home in forever."

"I'd laugh, but it's not funny. 'Cause now you know how I felt for years."

"Sorry about that. You have forgiven me for being thoughtless, haven't you?"

He knew the answer before he asked the question, but still felt a pang of guilt whenever the subject came up. Strange, how a child can have no problem at all being away from family. It doesn't mean they don't think about home, or Mom, or even a sibling. The child knows where he is, what he is doing, and that he is safe. Mothers, on the other hand, *need* the reassurance of a voice, or a letter, or something, to still the nightmares, and calm the runaway imagination, that something awful might have happened to their baby. Been that way for generations, and will more than likely continue for generations to come.

"Never crossed my mind not to," said Mom. "I love you, sweetie. And I look forward to Saturday."

"Same here."

With the thought still fresh in his head, Matt pushed speed dial 1, and waited for Jessica to answer.

But she didn't.

He left a brief message on her voicemail and returned to the balance of his day.

Chapter 9

He lies in wait near the villages; from ambush he murders the innocent
(Psalm 10:8 NIV).

JESSICA glanced at her phone and smiled. Too bad she couldn't put her camera down to answer this one. But she couldn't; so whatever Matthew needed to say, would have to wait. Made her heart skip a beat to think of him, though. Every time. Without fail.

Gazing through the lens of her latest acquisition, a top-of-the-line camera she had been admiring and saving for, for a year, her mind took her back to the date she'd had with Matt just before he moved to Dallas…

"I know it sounds crazy," he said. "But I'm a little nervous about starting a new job."

"You're kidding. After all you've been through, and the experience you have in a cockpit?"

"I said it sounds crazy."

"Well, I'm sorry about that. But I don't have much sympathy for you."

"Gee, thanks."

"Ok, I guess that was mean. But look at you. You're big and brave and gorgeous. All the co-pilots will be jealous; and all the female flight attendants will be after you. Doesn't sound like a bad job for a young, single man to me," she said with a chuckle.

She remembered the extended silence that followed that remark. Then she remembered Matthew turning in the seat to face her. They had parked down by the lake in Ransom Canyon to watch the moon reflected on the water. He looked at her for a long time.

"What?" she said, following an interminable silence.

"You really don't know, do you?"

"Know what? What am I missing?"

"Maybe it's too soon, and I should leave it alone."

Jessica scooted to the center of the seat and took his hand.

"Please don't."

Matt pushed the seat all the way back and lifted Jessica onto his lap. He kissed her, and kissed her good. She soared above the heavens; but quickly scrambled out of his lap—soon as she came to her senses. She had no intention of getting caught up in the moment and forgetting her name, or her place, or her responsibility as a Christian.

"Hold that thought," she said.

Grinning, he actually thanked her for slowing him down.

Oh yes. She would return his call, the second she finished covering the Tech football game, for the final time. Since the first Eunice Mae Howell article hit the stands, her phone had not stopped ringing, and her email inbox filled up weekly, with assignment offers. Plenty enough, so that Jessica felt confident in stepping down from her position at the *Journal* to take on bigger and more adventurous tasks.

Matt pushed "mute" on the television remote when he heard his phone buzz on the table next to his lounge chair.

"Hi, Jess! You okay? I was beginning to wonder if you had fallen off a cliff."

"Ha ha. I've been working, smarty pants. My last set of pictures covering a Texas Tech football game have been logged and digitally filed for tomorrow's paper. I'm pretty pumped about that."

"Your final game? What does that mean?"

"It means I have served my last day of a two-week notice and submitted my final package to the sports editor. So long *Avalanche Journal*."

Matt turned the TV off. No distraction should interrupt this conversation.

"So, you're moving to Dallas next week?"

"It could happen," she said with a laugh.

"I'd like that, you know."

"Really?"

"Cross my heart."

"That's a little sappy, coming from you."

Maybe so. But he meant what he said. He did want Jessica to move to Dallas. They could operate from the same hub; and might even be able to get to know one another better. He admired her spirit, her honesty, and her work ethic. The fact that her beauty took his breath away seemed entirely beside the point.

Plus, she'd been right. The flight attendants had been much too forward, for his taste. He needed the sweet presence of Jessica Roberts to keep the wolves at bay. And he would proudly walk with her on his arm—anywhere, anytime.

"I mean it, Jess. Please say you'll think about it."

"I think about it every day."

"Okay. Don't think; act."

"I'll see what I can do."

"In the meantime, are you doing anything Saturday night?"

"What did you have in mind?"

"Mom is playing at Reunion Tower and I'd like to take you. Like a real date. Ticket's on me, if you don't mind flying standby."

Jessica closed her eyes and leaned back in the office chair she would soon vacate for a final time. Fly to Dallas to see Matt. Did she have to think about it? Yes. But how could she say no? And what would happen after the concert? Where would she stay? What should she say?

"I would also book a room for you at the Anatole, where Mom is staying, if that would be okay."

The sentence worked like a soothing balm for her soul. Even Christians can easily be overcome with temptation. She just wasn't ready to put herself in that position. Didn't trust herself to be able to stop the momentum, once it got to rolling.

"Sounds wonderful. Will you be available to pick me up at the airport?"

"If not, I'll make sure Mom or Tommy picks you up. But I promise to try."

"You know, after all this time, I have yet to see your mother play in a live concert. I've only been present a few times when the family would get together and she'd play one-hit wonders or Christmas carols, or something. I'm super excited. Thank you. I'll have to buy a new dress, and a new pair of shoes, and."

"Woah! Don't put yourself in the poor house over this. I'm trying to make it fun, and keep the cost down for you."

"And I appreciate it. But I think I will ask Eunice Mae to go shopping with me."

For an instant, Jessica had thought she might ask Kim, but just as quickly remembered that, even though she and Kim had grown to be extremely close friends, they had completely different tastes in fashion. She loved Kim, and did not want to jeopardize their friendship over the likes of an outfit. She would definitely ask Eunice Mae.

"Couldn't ask for a better guide, when it comes to a classy wardrobe."

"I know. And I think she will enjoy the chance to tell someone what to do. She doesn't get much opportunity for that anymore."

Jessica drank in the sound of Matt's voice as they chatted on for a while about their individual lives and careers, and what might come next for both of them. They discussed housing options in the Dallas area, according to Matt's experience and information he had acquired from other pilots. They talked weather and politics and family, until midnight.

"Guess I better get some shut-eye if I'm going to be worth anything tomorrow," she finally said.

"Yeah, me, too," said Matt. "I have a ten o'clock flight in the morning."

"Then hang up the phone and go to bed," said Jessica.

His laughter brought a fresh smile to her lips as he said, "Yes, ma'am."

"Sorry. Don't want anyone dying on my account."

"Not to worry."

Sleep came for Jessica after much personal debate. The notion of making Dallas her home base—the city where Matthew Baldwin lived—kept her blood pumping. But she had family in Lubbock. And Ms. Eunice. What would she do without Eunice Mae close by?

"You're over-thinking the whole situation," she mumbled to herself as she turned over in the bed.

She began to pray, asking for guidance, for that still small voice to say, "This is the way; walk in it."

At long last, she drifted off, the slightest hint of a grin, still on her face.

Jessica stood at the luggage carousel watching for the bright pink artificial flower she had tied securely to the handle of her suitcase. Lost in concentration, she paid no attention to the man who planted himself next to her, until she felt a firm hand on her elbow.

She looked up into the face of a stranger. A stranger with dark, foreboding eyes, who reeked of tobacco and alcohol.

"Get your hands off me before I scream," she said in a low growl, as she jerked her elbow out of his grasp.

The foreboding man grabbed her upper arm, and held on with a vise-like grip. "You don't want to do that, lady. I have a man standing by at your sweetheart's house, waiting for word from me to take him out. You need to cooperate, or he will be dead before you have time to scream."

Jessica looked around for a way out of this dilemma; but with a quick glance down at his left hand, she noticed a cell phone, ready to push SEND, to a number with an area code she couldn't identify. Someone had Matt in their gun sights? What would this man do to her if she went with him? If she didn't?

"Can I at least get my luggage?" she said. "I need my medication."

At that moment, Jessica's suitcase rolled in front of her. Like a hand had plucked it out of the lineup and placed it there, at exactly the right second.

"It's right there," she said, reaching for it.

The stinky man held her back, but pocketed his cell phone and reached for the luggage. He rolled it along behind him with one hand and kept a tight grip on her elbow with the other. She couldn't think of a way out, so she went along with him. What if he had told the truth; and Matt really was in danger? Curiosity ate at her, though. Matt hadn't been in Dallas that long, and she couldn't imagine a punk like this knowing about their relationship. Something didn't fit. But what could she do? She certainly couldn't wrestle him to the ground and get away. He towered over her. And there was the threat to consider. Maybe he was a jerk from Matthew's past. Someone who held a grudge for some unknown reason. Someone who had connections somewhere, or knew someone who knew someone, who knew them both. Some seedy character with malice in his heart, and no proper outlet with which to deal with it.

All Jessica could think to do was to pray, and believe that God would protect Matt, and send someone to her rescue.

Outside the terminal a plain, white panel van waited at the curb. The stinky man walked up to the van and tapped on the sliding door three times. Someone inside slid the side panel open and the kidnapper shoved Jessica inside.

Simultaneously, Tommy Churchwell pulled alongside the curb behind them. Traffic had caused a delay in his getting to the airport to meet Jessica. He stared in disbelief as he watched Jessica being forced into the van. He pulled out his cell phone and dialed 911 first then speed-dialed Matt, then Catherine.

"Yes, I'm tailing them," said Tommy. "If you don't hear from me in a couple hours, go on to the concert. Soon as this is over, I'll meet you there."

"I'll pray that this nightmare is over long before I have to be at Reunion Tower," said Catherine. "And if it isn't, I'll cancel the whole thing. I'll get off the line now, so you can stay in touch with the police."

"Thanks, Babe. Don't let up on the prayers. Love you."

Tommy returned to the 911 operator and gave her a blow-by-blow description of every turn the white van made, every road sign he could read, and every detail he could remember about the man who had taken Jessica. The van did not have a license plate or any distinguishing features. No words painted on the side, either, so he had to keep up with it in a sea of other vehicles.

The van sped up Highway 97 to 121 then made a sharp turn onto 635 at Coppell. Traffic on 635 worked against the driver of the van, however, and he slowed way down then finally had to stop altogether. Tommy could see the accident down the road that had caused the traffic jam. But his truck was too far back. He wouldn't be able to get the attention of the police officer at the scene of the accident. With the freeway at a standstill, Tommy made a hasty, selfless decision. He didn't take time to think about what he was doing—just slammed the gear shift knob toward PARK and jumped out, headed straight for the white van. He ran, screaming as he went, arms waving over his head, praying someone would hear, would care, would help.

The sun peeked out through heavy cloud cover, bringing hope that a thunderstorm wouldn't further complicate the situation.

With the van just a few car lengths ahead, a tall, broad man, wearing a white Stetson jumped out of a 4x4, four-door black Ford 250 carrying a pistol out in front of him, and joined Tommy in pursuit. The man didn't ask questions, didn't seem to think Tommy was crazy, just moved forward with him, seemingly determined to help.

Still two car lengths behind the kidnapper van, Tommy noticed that the driver of the van had slammed into the car directly behind him, and was turning toward the service lane.

"Follow me!" yelled the stranger, moving ahead with long strides. He hurried along the freeway in black cowboy boots, as easily as if he wore running shoes. He seemed confident and certain of his next move, and Tommy did not hesitate to follow his lead.

Tommy kicked up his efforts and soon caught up with the big man. Just as the van started into the service lane, the stranger aimed and fired, once. He must have hit his mark, because the van came to a sudden halt, with the back right tire blown out. The van was still only for a moment then limped forward, and started gaining speed.

Tommy stared in amazement as this tall stranger, who looked like he'd just stepped out of a western movie, didn't hesitate, but fired another round into the left rear tire. He raced forward and shot out the right front, crouched low in front of the van, and shot out the left front, then stood to his full height and raised his weapon, pointed directly at the driver.

"Get out of the van!" he shouted. "Now!"

The passenger door opened, and a dark-haired man tumbled out. He threw his weapon on the ground and raised his hands in surrender. Amazing. The driver scrambled out behind the first man. Several men from nearby vehicles jumped on the two men and pinned them to the pavement. The tall stranger came back around the van, and made his way to the side panel door. He banged on it with the barrel of his gun. Tommy watched in amazement.

"Come out with your hands up!"

The panel slid open, and a man with a shaved head appeared. But before he could say or do anything, his body came flying out of the van head first, and landed at the stranger's feet. The tall stranger looked up in surprise and saw Jessica Roberts, wrists and ankles still bound with duct tape, her mouth taped shut, staring back at him. Her feet were still poised in the form she had taken to push her captor out of the van. Fire flashed in her eyes, even as tears poured down her face.

"Jessica?" said Tommy, pushing past the crowd that had gathered. "Are you hurt?"

Jessica's eyebrows rose as though to demonstrate her inability to respond.

Tommy scrambled up into the van and crawled over to her. He ripped the tape off her mouth in one swift motion.

"No, I'm not hurt," she said, struggling to breathe. She pointed to the right with her head. "But please." Deep breath. "Get my inhaler." Deep breath. "My bag is. Back there."

Tommy scooted to the back of the van, through debris and empty bottles, holding his breath to subdue the stench. He found Jessica's bag, dug out the inhaler then dragged the bag back with him.

In the meantime, the stranger in the white hat leaned into the van and cut the tape off Jessica's wrists and ankles.

"Thank you," said Jessica. "Thank you both. I was scared there for a while."

"My name is Tommy Churchwell," said Tommy, extending his hand toward the stranger. "I can't imagine what might have happened, without your help."

"Right place, right time," he said. "Name's Bill Steed, Texas Ranger. Glad to be of service."

"Nice to meet you. This is Jessica Roberts, a…"

"I know that name," said Bill. "Saw the article in *Time* magazine. I bet that Eunice Mae Howell was a force to be reckoned with back in the '40's."

Jessica laughed. "She still is."

She used the inhaler one more time then she and Tommy climbed down out of the van.

The second Jessica's head emerged the growing crowd broke into thunderous applause and cheers. Traffic stood still long after the fender-bender ahead of them had been cleared away. As they stood around thinking about their next move, Tommy's phone sang a tune from his pocket.

"I was just about to call you," said Tommy. "Yes, she's fine. A little shaken, but unharmed."

The whir of helicopter blades cut the conversation short. Tommy looked up to see Matt waving at him from inside the helicopter. Tommy lifted his arms in a questioning manner. "Had to see for myself!" cried Matt with the aid of an air horn. "I'll meet you at the police station!"

Jessica looked up and gave Matt a big, broad smile, and waved her arm from side to side over her head; and didn't stop waving until the helicopter had left her line of vision.

Jessica settled into the passenger seat of Tommy's pickup truck. She held her hands together in her lap to control their trembling. Earlier, anger and fear had fed her adrenaline, tempered only by prayer. But now that the crisis had passed and the men who had taken her were in custody, the facts came at her, hard.

She had been abducted by three men. She had no idea who they were or what their motivation might be. They had indicated that her "sweetheart" was being held at gunpoint, but had not mentioned a name. What if she could have attracted attention to them in the airport and avoided the entire incident? But what if, by some wild stretch of the imagination, someone really did have Matt held captive somewhere; and suppose she could have been insanely, directly, unequivocally responsible for his death? Just the thought of it made her shiver.

"You okay?" said Tommy.

Jessica turned toward Matthew's stepfather.

"I am now. I think. Or I will be, anyway. It's the first time I've ever been kidnapped."

"I can only imagine."

"I'm so grateful you were there, and didn't hesitate to follow the van. Thank you."

"You're welcome."

The ride to the police station didn't take long, and Jessica held all the other thoughts in her heart, pondering whether the men who had held her actually knew anything at all about her, about Matt. Obviously, they hadn't held Matthew at gunpoint, or he would not have appeared above the traffic jam in a helicopter. Had she just been a random target? What had they planned to do with her, if Tommy and the Texas ranger had not interrupted their plan?

Whatever their motives, they had failed to complete the task. Jessica shuddered, closed her eyes, and praised God, once again, for sending help, at just the right moment, in just the right way.

Chapter 10

You came near when I called you, and you said, "Do not fear." You, Lord, took up my case; you redeemed my life (Lamentations 3:57-58 NIV).

AT THE police station, Jessica gave her statement to a detective.

"Thank you, Miss Roberts," said Detective Burk. "We have informed the FBI that the men who kidnapped you have been apprehended. We have been working a joint effort operation to bring them to justice for quite some time. They're street thugs who have been pulling this stunt at the airport every other month or so. They changed up so often, we couldn't nail down a routine well enough to catch them. I'd say you are very fortunate. The other four ladies who disappeared from the airport did not live to tell the tale. Dallas County will sleep better tonight, knowing this group of cutthroats is behind bars. Looks to me like you owe Mr. Churchwell here a huge debt of gratitude."

Jessica cut her eyes toward Tommy, and the waterworks began, in earnest. All the emotions she had kept bottled up inside since the moment she'd been taken came rushing to the surface. She covered her face with her hands, and her shoulders shook with the sobbing.

Tommy moved to stand beside her, just as Matthew Baldwin burst through the front door of the station. They could hear his voice all the way back in the interrogation room.

"Where is Jessica Roberts?"

"I'll get him," said Tommy with a smile and a squeeze of Jessica's shoulder.

"We're right behind you," said Detective Burk. "We have all the information we need for now."

Jessica rallied and followed Detective Burk and Tommy out of the office and down the hall to the left. When Jessica appeared at the end of the hallway, Matt sucked in a deep breath then took one cautious step forward, concern evident in his eyes.

"I'm fine," said Jessica, wiping the last trace of tears with the back of her hand. "Really. I've had a minute to calm down."

Jessica stuck out her arms, twisted them in the air, showing the front then the back. She turned a full circle, to show she had no injuries. "See, perfectly fine."

Matt opened his arms to her, and instantly knew she wasn't one hundred percent fine. Her shoulders began to shake and the tears to fall. She had been kidnapped by a trio of serial killers; of course she wasn't fine.

Holding her close with his left hand, Matt reached out his other toward Tommy. "Don't know how to thank you, sir."

"You just did. And it wasn't just me. We owe Jessica's ultimate safety to Ranger Steed. I'd like to thank him, but don't know where he disappeared to."

Matthew had admired and respected Tommy for years. But those feelings paled in comparison with how he felt at the present moment. No question about it, he had saved Jessica's life, Ranger Steed notwithstanding. Wow.

A breeze drifted through the room. Tommy grinned big, so Matt turned to see what had caught his attention.

Beautiful as an angel, Matt's mother glided into the room. Dressed for the concert scheduled for that evening, she really did resemble an angel—with her hair still long and flowing, and her glittered gown, snowy white, swirling softly at her feet.

"Mother, what are you doing here?"

"Where else would I be? Soon as Tommy called I caught a cab over here." She rushed to Jessica's side. "Are you all right, sweetie? What a nightmare for you. Of course, I do not expect you to attend a silly old concert after what you've been through. And I didn't want to miss the opportunity to see you. I had to make sure for myself that you were unharmed."

Matt had not been altogether surprised to see his mother. All the years she had been his mother, she had been the same. She cared about people, and didn't hesitate to show it. And she had a soft spot for Jessica, who had been Kim's best friend since she had set foot on Texas soil, had stood by her through some frightening and lonely months. Naturally, Catherine would do whatever it took to keep tabs on one she considered as one of her own. Marilyn would have done the same for Kim. And Matt knew it.

Jessica's answer, however, did surprise him.

"I was terribly frightened," said Jessica. "I don't deny that. But right now, I think a concert sounds perfect. Do I have time to change and get decent?"

"Of course you do, if that's what you want."

"Are you sure?" said Matt.

"Totally sure. I'd like to have something beautiful to take my mind off the ugly."

Catherine's skilled hands worked their magic. As Jessica closed her eyes and listened, the trauma of the afternoon melted away. After all, the bad guys were behind bars and wouldn't hurt another human being for a long, long time. What did she have to fear?

Nothing. Absolutely nothing.

Jessica glanced down to see Matt's hand wrapped warmly around her own, even while his eyes remained fixed on his mother. A grin had replaced the concentrated frown from earlier in the day. Her feelings for him had begun to grow, headed toward full-blown love.

The idea made her nervous. Matt hadn't been home all that long; he had never made a long-term commitment to anyone; and he had never indicated a desire to do so. But maybe she wouldn't have to worry about that. Maybe everything would work out perfectly. Perhaps her knight in shining armor would remove the metal jacket and share the real-life man with her. Maybe. For now, she would choose to believe. A definite possibility.

So far, they had not had a cross word. So far, they had both put their best foot forward. And then there was her career, his career, her geographic location, and his geographic location. Something good could come of their union. One day. She would pray, and wait for such a day.

For now, she could only dream how real life would be should they choose to live it out together, as one flesh, one love, for life. The future would bring what the future would bring. But today, she would put such thoughts aside and absorb the blessings afforded in their current relationship—the way it is today.

Might near perfect.

Jessica whispered goodbye when she disembarked the plane at Lubbock Preston Smith International Airport. The tall, handsome pilot had stepped out of the cockpit, just for this moment. Jessica's heart swelled with pride. She had been completely aware that all eyes followed her as she approached the front of the aircraft. Especially the eyes of two, now hopeless flight attendants who had each made attempts to persuade Matthew Baldwin to share a night on the town. They were now being forced to witness the reason they had both been shut down, without a prayer.

Much to her surprise, Matt went so far as to kiss her cheek before he released her hand to lead the other passengers into the covered walkway. She could feel the heat in her cheeks, and the grin would stay affixed to her face for the next several hours. Her feelings for him had grown over the past few months, and she felt sure his feelings for her had expanded as well. They hadn't said the "L" word out loud yet, but she knew it was coming. And right now, looking up into his eyes, she was totally okay with that.

Matt had another flight out, so no time to visit; but Jessica had not had the final surprise of the day. When she stepped out into the open area near the luggage claim rack, she looked up to see Kim standing there.

Kim raced toward her. "Are you okay? Mom called me before the concert and told me all about it. I had to come."

"Oh, Kim. Thank you. It's so good to see you. I'm glad you could get away. Being in an airport alone again so soon, seemed a little creepy. Even here in Lubbock, where I shouldn't be afraid of anything."

Kimberly Baldwin, attorney at law. The two of them didn't get to see near enough of one another since each embarking on active careers that demanded so much of their time.

"You must have been scared half out of your wits. Come on. I'll wait with you till your luggage gets here. I assume your car is somewhere in long-term parking."

Jessica had been gone a total of 72 hours; but it seemed more like a week. And now she was home, at last. It helped her nerves, knowing Kim would be here with her. She smiled at her friend.

"Yeah, it's pretty far out. I left on a busy weekend, I guess."

"No worries. I'll give you a lift out to it. Would you care to join me for dinner? I've got chicken in the crockpot, and we could bake a couple of sweet potatoes. I know you like them. And I have one of those delicious, prepackaged salads in the fridge. I know it sounds wrong, but I've been so busy at work I didn't take time to prepare a proper meal. But we could watch a sappy movie, make popcorn and drink Cokes, and you could get acclimated to what normal feels like."

"Sounds perfect. Thanks."

The two of them made a night of it. Jessica answered all of Kim's questions about the kidnapping and the concert, and she even opened up a little about her growing feelings for Matt.

"He's really something, your brother," said Jessica.

"I know," said Kim. "He scared Mother half to death the whole time he was growing up. But it looks like he may be ready to settle down a little, and act like a normal human being."

"Maybe," said Jessica. "But he will never fit the mold of normal."

What she didn't say, was a lot. Like how her heart leapt into her throat every time she saw Matthew Baldwin. How easily she got lost in his eyes, and how breathless he left her after a kiss.

"Yeah," said Jessica. "Your brother is really something."

The grin had once again attached itself to her face. Matthew Baldwin could change her life forever.

Was she ready for that?

A solid month dragged by before the second article on Eunice Mae Howell appeared in *Time* magazine. An international crisis had taken precedence over the lovely Lubbock celebrity. But today, at long last, her story would continue.

Chapter 11

The wise prevail through great power, and those who have knowledge muster their strength. Surely you need guidance to wage war, and victory is won through many advisers (Proverbs 24:5-6 NIV).

JUST AS before, Matt bought every copy of the current *Time* magazine at the newsstand perched inside the airport. He traveled through the shops and the food court, snatching up copies wherever he could find them. He saved some for family who may have missed opening day, then proceeded to give them away to everyone he deemed worthy, and especially to his contacts in the news reporting or publishing field who might be able to give Jessica's career a boost.

His strategy worked. Jessica got busy; and then she got gone. More and more of her assignments sent her to foreign countries for weeks at a time. Back-to-back assignments that kept them apart. Their date nights had dwindled to less than once or twice in a six-week period. The old Matt would have been relieved not to have a woman under foot all the time. But since meeting Jessica Roberts, his attitude had changed—considerably.

Matt had developed serious feelings for this small, beautiful girl who had captured his heart. A full twelve inches measured the difference in their stature; he stood tall and broad at the shoulders, while she seemed to be a mere whisper of a girl. But not a weak, sickly, skinny girl. Jessica worked out every day, sported well-formed calves and small, but muscular arms. Her assignments often found her in rugged terrain; but she managed to give as good as she got, when it came to battling the elements.

Matt had settled into the quaint atmosphere of a small coffee shop, reading Jessica's latest article on Ms. Eunice Mae Howell. Fascinated. Near the end of the article, he felt a presence standing in front of the small table, and this person did not make a move to leave.

Annoyed, Matt set the magazine down on the table and frowned up at the intruder. He opened his mouth to voice his disdain, but instantly snapped it shut again.

"Jessica."

"In the flesh," she said, with a grin. "Is this seat taken?"

"No, no," said Matt, recovering. He jumped up and pulled the chair out for her.

Jessica laughed. As if she couldn't pull the chair out for herself. Matt knew the thought behind the snicker; but he couldn't help himself. She seemed to bring out the best in him. And he did not apologize.

"What brings you here?" he said.

He didn't really care about the answer. The point was she had come on her own volition. Apparently, she wanted to see him; and it had not required any prompting from him. He loved that.

"Well, I've been looking all over the airport for a copy of *Time* magazine; and everyone told me I needed to find you before I'd have any luck."

She laughed again, and his heart did a somersault in his chest.

"Guilty as charged," he said, pointing to the stack beside the table. His posture relaxed, his mind at ease with her. "I was almost through reading your latest article, before I was interrupted."

"You'll have plenty of time to read in about four days."

Matt's ears perked up, like a puppy. What was she about to say? Four days with Jessica would be heaven on earth. He decided to play it cool, rein in his emotions, and mask the shout that wanted to escape through the portals to his soul.

"Why is that?" he said, with all the calm he could muster. "Am I going on vacation?"

"Probably not," said Jessica. "Although I would take you with me if I could."

There went the air out of that balloon.

"Where are you off to next?"

He held his breath, afraid of what she might say.

"Not too far. Paris, France."

"For how long?"

"Looks like two weeks, right now."

Did he dare ask what political upheaval had happened since yesterday that would require the expertise of an excellent photo journalist? How much danger would she be in? Would he be looking at another two weeks without sleep?

"Will you be in danger?" He couldn't help it; he had to ask.

"I hope not. Fashion Week begins September 27th. I thought the hoopla and all the colors and crazy fashions might be fun. I could use a light-weight assignment. After Israel."

A rush of air escaped as Matt realized he had been holding his breath. He had spent three weeks of long nights, praying for Jessica while she was on assignment in Israel. Anything could have happened to her over there. Anything. And a lot of it, not good.

"How long have you been back?"

Another challenge in this relationship. Jessica had been so independent, Matt often did not know where she went, or when she came home, unless he picked up the phone and called her mother.

He made an effort to focus on Jessica, as she answered his question.

"I took a week off to spend with family and do some tweaking on the next Eunice Mae article. And I expect to take another few days to hang around in Dallas searching for an apartment, and waiting for your next day off. If my informant was right, you are free for the next two days, and I wanted to see you before I flew out again."

What did she say? Dallas. Searching for an apartment. His hopes were beginning to climb.

"When do you leave?"

"Next Tuesday."

Next Tuesday. More time than they had ever had together in one stretch. If only he could make it work out that way.

"Let's see," he said. "Today is Thursday. I know someone who owes me a favor so I'm sure I can be available the entire time you're here. My prayers have finally been answered with a yes. So, let me help you look, then help you move. It would be the nicest big change in my life for a good long time."

Jessica began to second-guess herself. Four days in the company of Matt Baldwin. Could she trust herself not to throw herself at him? She had been missing him something fierce lately. Long lonely assignments, for weeks at a time, could not be completely filled with work. Thoughts often came unbidden—his eyes, his voice, the memory of a kiss. The way he treated her like a lady, ever patient, ever waiting. Giving her the space she needed to chase a career. Yeah, she had missed him.

But how could everything she owned be moved such a long distance in such a small amount of time? Jessica grinned at herself. It wouldn't be that difficult, really. Everything was already packed. The close call she'd had at Love Field not so long ago, then the assignment in Israel that had taken her closer to a war zone than she'd ever thought she'd be, combined to make her realize how much it would mean to her to be closer in proximity to Matt. Close enough to go out for dinner when they both happened to be in town. Close enough to hang out for a day, attend his mother's piano concerts together, and just know they shared the same zip code. Close enough to develop a meaningful relationship. Close enough to fall in love. Deeply, truly, eternally, in love.

But Jessica would not spend four days with Matt Baldwin, or move her belongings from Lubbock to Dallas, or fly to Paris to cover Fashion Week. *USA Today* had seen her coverage of Israel, and had offered a hurry-up-this-can't-wait assignment—to Afghanistan.

A knock at the door. Jessica closed the lid on her suitcase but didn't bother to remove it from the bed. She moved to the door, opened it, and immediately felt her heart sink.

Matthew. She hadn't told him yet, and dreaded the conversation. For both of them.

"Afghanistan," said Matt, a frown creasing his brow. "Right on the heels of Israel? Are you sure that's wise, Jess?"

He had no right to question her judgment; he knew that. He could only think of what might happen to her over there, his own memories still a source to be contended with. She could be abducted, tortured, killed.

"Maybe not," she said. "But it's my job and I feel an obligation to tell the story."

Matt frowned deeper, unsure how far he should take this line of questioning. His words alone would not sway her. But he'd been there, and still battled the pictures in his memory. Would she be safe? Could she be safe? Did the people sending her over there have a clue what she might be walking into?

Matt ran a hand over his face and moved to sit on the loveseat beneath the window. A few seconds later, Jessica joined him. He took her hand in his, rubbed his thumb across the back of it.

"You're going, no matter what I say, aren't you?"

"Yes," she whispered, looking straight into his eyes.

And she did. At three in the afternoon, on the day he thought she would be signing a lease. On the day before he thought he would be moving her, lock, stock, and barrel, to Dallas.

And she couldn't give him a definite return date.

The images swirled in her head as Jessica curled up under the thin woolen blanket and prayed for peace. She had taken the assignment mostly out of curiosity. She had to admit that. And she didn't feel very noble at the moment. Tonight, she longed for home, her own bed, the sound of her mother's voice. The love she had grown to recognize in Matt's eyes.

The boy had been somewhere between the ages of ten and twelve, if her guess could be relied upon. Jessica had stepped out from behind a crumbling wall just in time to see the young boy take the rifle off a fallen American soldier and aim it at the Marine who stood between herself and the ravages of war.

The Marine had had no choice, really. The boy would have killed someone, and it could have been her. He told her later, that would not happen on his watch.

It wasn't supposed to be this way. Her assignment did not specify reporting in a combat zone. But things hadn't gone as planned. The platoon that had been directed to guard her had been caught in the crossfire of a renegade band that seemed to have come out of nowhere. The platoon sergeant ordered her to disguise herself in fatigues, to stay low, and to remain in the company of a marine. At all times. She had tried to obey. And now she found herself staring at a young man, wielding a rifle, who couldn't be much more than ten years old. A child thrown into war.

Jessica would never forget the look of pure hatred in the young man's eyes as he raised the gun to fire. But more than that, the dead eyes that lay still in his head, and the blood that covered his chest, would remain with her forever.

Scene after scene passed through her mind. Children under the age of five, killed as falling rocks from bomb-blasted buildings landed on them, and the adults who carried dead children in their arms through the streets. The memories kept sleep at bay, night after night.

But now, after a month of dodging the enemy and unforeseen challenges, one more long, grueling day and she would fly back to the States. Most of her, anyway. She would leave a piece of her heart in Afghanistan. The piece that broke and fell at her feet as she gazed upon the ruin and rubble of men, women and children, who fought for their lives every day. She felt certain many of them had no idea why such tragedy had fallen upon their little village, in a vast country full of war and famine and fear.

Surely she could wait one more day.

The copy she wrote to accompany each picture pulled at her soul, leaving her in emotional shreds.

At the end of the four-week assignment, one day stretched into five as heavy fighting made it impossible for the helicopter to get her out. The sights and sounds kept her on her knees in prayer—even as she ran, weighted down with equipment, through the streets, hiding behind buildings that had once stood five and ten stories high, she prayed.

At last, on the morning of November 1st, the helicopter came for her. As the chopper lifted off the ground and carried her away from danger, she finally let her emotions release. Prayers of praise and thanksgiving ascended, and tears flowed, washing her heart, her mind, her soul, of the images that plagued her, so she could finally believe she was going home.

Many travel-hours later, the United States glowed beautiful below her. Jessica had managed to rest, meditate, and organize the Afghanistan story, order the pictures, and come up with an outline for the finished article. She'd had plenty of time. She couldn't sleep anyway—not without disturbing dreams that put her right back into the throes of war.

Jessica's rescue flight landed at DFW Airport approximately 8,000 miles later, and she felt her face break out into a very grateful, very broad smile. Gathered around the baggage claim station stood Matt, his mother and stepfather, Kimberly, Ms. Eunice, and Jessica's own mother. Jessica had managed to get word out regarding the delay, and each change of flight times throughout the hours. She had intended for everyone to know she was okay; but had not expected this kind of a reception.

She did not have to choose which person to run to first. They surrounded her in one big swarm. Everyone crying and laughing and shouting at the same time.

Home. She would never take it for granted again. Never.

Matt Baldwin had called in every favor he could remember that anyone, anywhere, owed him. He had pulled more strings than he knew he had access to. Even Ms. Eunice came forward and contacted the men and women in the military she had built relationships with through the years. Matt felt sure Jessica would never know how much noise had been made, pushing people to get her out of Afghanistan. Even with the government and the media working together, it had still taken five long, nightmarish days to get the job done.

The military wanted Jessica safely out of Afghanistan too. They didn't need a civilian casualty to put a spotlight on them. In a spirit of cooperation, they maneuvered around battles until they found a way out. Although they appreciated her willingness to make the realities of war more clear for the American citizens, they also bore the burden of keeping a civilian safe in what had turned out to be a war zone.

As Matt watched Jessica now, seated across from him at Desperado's, his heart squeezed with love for this tiny, brave, stubborn, confident, cherished woman. She could have been killed over there, and lost to him forever.

He determined, right then, to do something to take their relationship to the next level. If she lived in Dallas, would he have some influence on what assignments she accepted, and where they might be geographically located?

Sure you would, Matt. Jessica is a very independent woman, and I think you know better than that. But I still expect you to try. Who knows? She might be open to the idea.

It was a nice thought, anyway. Matt smiled across the table at Jessica. She noticed, and returned the gesture. But her eyes looked glassy and tired. He recognized that look. Had felt the effects more than once. Jet lag. She must be anxious to get some sleep. They had all wanted to see her so badly they hadn't considered her level of exhaustion.

"Listen up, people," he said, tapping his fork on the side of his glass. "I think it's time we wind down this party and let Jessica get some rest."

Everyone spoke at the same time, in agreement.

"I hope you don't mind, I took the liberty of getting us a room," said Marilyn. "We can bunk together for one night, don't you think? It's a room with two queen-size beds."

Jessica smiled at her mother, moved to her very soul with appreciation. Jessica knew her mother very well, knew she had been loved unconditionally since the moment of her birth. Even after Jessica's father left them alone, and without provision, Marilyn had stepped up into the helm of the ship and grasped the wheel that would steer the direction of their lives until Jessica disembarked and began making her own way.

And now, alone and uncertain every time Jessica accepted another assignment, she knew her mother had prayed for her. She encouraged her, and accepted her life choices without criticism or strife. Jessica had recalled her mother's words on more than one occasion as she maneuvered through her adult life. "I appreciate the fact that my mother rarely gave unsolicited advice. I knew she prayed for me every day, and then left me in God's hands. I was one of His children, you see, and Mother had been wise enough to know God would make a much better parent for me than any earthly man or woman. My goal has always been to be that kind of mother to you, Jess."

Her mother's words came to mind again, and Jessica smiled at her across the table, a genuine smile that was meant to convey the love in her heart.

"I don't mind at all. Sounds wonderful. And I am a little beat, at that. My eyes are getting heavy. I had a little trouble sleeping on the flight. Couldn't get my brain to slow down."

Tommy paid the check and stood to pull out Catherine's chair. Matt put his hand at Jessica's elbow and guided her toward the door, with Marilyn, Kim, and Ms. Eunice right behind them.

Outside, Matt walked Jessica to her mother's car, wrapped his arms around her, and planted a kiss on top of her head.

"I am so glad you are home safe from that dreadful place."

"Thank you," mumbled Jessica, into his shirt.

He stepped back and looked down at her.

"It's gonna take a while to get over this one," she said.

"You have access to all the support you need. Call me when you feel rested and we'll talk. Ok?"

"Thanks again."

"Ready?" said Marilyn.

"Yes, ma'am," said Jessica.

"I'll talk to you soon," said Matt. "Sleep soundly, and have only good dreams. You're home safe now. Remember that."

"I'm certainly going to try," she said. "If I can turn this brain off."

Chapter 12

Let us then approach God's throne of grace with confidence, so that we may receive mercy and find grace to help us in our time of need (Hebrews 4:16 NIV).

ONE WEEK after her return from Afghanistan, Jessica flew back to Lubbock, courtesy of Southwest Airlines. Marilyn and Kim had returned to Lubbock the day after their welcome-home dinner. But Jessica had stayed over to rest, to get past the jet lag, and spend a little time with Matt.

Unwilling to face the apartment filled with packed boxes, Jessica spent only a few minutes there, gathering a few additional outfits. She had agreed to stay with her mother for a while, until she felt ready to be alone again.

Jessica woke with a start, disoriented and covered in sweat, the nightmares a little too real.

"Dear Lord," she whispered, "please subdue these memories so I can rest. But at the same time, I don't want to forget what I experienced over there. I realize I should continue to pray for the innocent. The victims. And even the bad guys. But I'm so exhausted."

Jessica stared at the ceiling, tears slipping softly down the sides of her face and pooling in her ears. If she kept her eyes open, she could hold the pictures at bay. But she couldn't sleep with her eyes open.

Exasperated, Jessica swung her feet to the floor and headed toward the bedroom door, in the home she'd been raised in. Marilyn had pleaded with her not to go back to her apartment until she felt more stable, more rested, more in control, and she had agreed. Just knowing someone would be there if she needed someone to talk to, meant a lot.

Jessica knew the way to the kitchen without turning on any lights. She tiptoed down the long hall then turned at the living room toward the kitchen.

Her toe bumped into something firm. Something not where it belonged. Her eyes adjusted to the dim light and she found her mother kneeling in front of the couch. Jessica reached over to turn on the lamp.

"Mother, are you okay? What's wrong?"

Jessica lowered herself to the floor next to her mother. Tears flowed. Her mother's eyes were red. Her shoulders shook.

Jessica waited, one hand on her mother's shoulder.

"What in the world did you go through over there, Jessica?" her mother said at last. "I heard your nightmares, but I was afraid to wake you up. Couldn't think of anything else to do, but pray. I do my Bible study in here, and I felt like God would know I meant business if I came to this spot to pray for your peace."

Jessica had no idea what sounds she made during the nightmares. But her mom was badly shaken, so they must be disturbing.

"Oh," said Jessica. She took her mother's hands in her own, and said, "I'm sorry, Mother. I did see some terrible things in Afghanistan, but I was never personally treated badly. Children are dying over there, who should be in a pristine white nursery school. It broke my heart. The sights and sounds of war are hard to leave behind. But I'm fine. Really. It will just take some time."

The image of her mother crying and praying on her behalf would stay with Jessica for a lifetime. She felt grateful and guilty at the same time.

Grateful that her mother loved her, and had sacrificed any personal dreams and goals she may have once had, to properly raise her daughter. They had attended church services on a regular basis, since before Jessica had been born. Marilyn had seen to it that Jessica spent her summers in wholesome church camps or sports camps, or working a job. Much of Jessica's work ethic had grown from watching her mother support the two of them, sometimes under the pressure of excessive hardship, but always with great personal satisfaction and reward.

And guilt, because Jessica had not always taken the safe route, made the smartest choices, or fallen for the most upright of gentlemen. Yet her mother's love and devotion had never wavered.

Jessica shook off the image and the memories, and forced herself to focus on the computer screen in front of her face. She had been back home for a week, and had a deadline to meet, no matter what ghosts she might have to deal with. The newspaper would just grant her so much time. It was her first job with them, and she didn't want it to be the last.

Jessica had only unpacked the necessities for survival, in the kitchen and bath rooms. She had work to do; and would deal with the majority of the apartment on another day.

Three hours later, Jessica pushed SEND. The final version of the Afghanistan article, now on its way to *USA Today*—her first national newspaper publication. The article would be published in two separate releases, due to the volume of words and the number of pictures. The first would be released the week after article three on the life of Eunice Mae Howell.

Jessica tucked away the printed version of the Afghanistan story, closed her laptop, and stretched out on the sofa for a nap. She had been back in the States long enough to finally begin getting a handle on days and nights, sleeping and eating at the right time, and dealing with the aftermath of her experience in Afghanistan.

She pulled a throw pillow under her right cheek and closed her eyes. Almost immediately her cell phone buzzed on the coffee table. She opened one eye, picked it up, and saw that Eunice Mae was calling. Jessica didn't hesitate to take the call.

"Yes, ma'am. What can I do for you?"

"I've called 911. Would you meet us at Covenant?"

"Of course, I will. What's going on?"

"Just feeling a little heavy in my chest. Thought I'd better get it checked out. There's the doorbell, sweetie. I'll see you at the hospital."

"I'm on my way."

Jessica grabbed a windbreaker from the closet by the door, and her keys and purse off the entry table then headed out. On the way, she called Catherine and Kim. She would call Matt after they knew more. He was too far away to bother, especially if it came to nothing. All of her own discomforts instantly melted away. The life of her friend could be hanging in the balance. *Pray, Jessica. Pray for God's favor. Pray for the health and well-being of Eunice Mae Howell.* "She still has much to give, Lord," Jessica prayed aloud. "I still have much to learn from her. Please don't take her home yet. Please, Jesus, amen."

Then she remembered her warrior skills as a Christian. She had recently been studying on the subject and decided to give it a try.

"I bind you, Satan, in the name of Jesus," she declared. "You have no power here. I command you and your minions to be gone from the body of Eunice Mae Howell, and the room where she is resting. I bind any harm you may have had in mind for her, Satan, and order you, in the name of Jesus, to be gone!"

Jessica, Catherine, Tommy and Kimberly gathered in the emergency room waiting area.

"She's 90 years old, I realize," said Jessica. "But she's no ordinary 90-year-old. She's very healthy, only takes vitamins and supplements, no meds. Eats organic everything. Her only vice, if you could call it that, is a cup of coffee every morning, from beans she grinds herself. I hope she will be okay. No, I trust God that she will be okay. She's a believer, you know, and has probably set Satan to rights already."

They prayed and talked quietly together for an hour before Dr. Forester entered the waiting room. "The Howell family?"

"We are Eunice Mae's family," said Catherine, standing to her feet.

That's exactly who they were. Eunice Mae Howell had immediately become a surrogate member of the family the moment she and Maggie had become fast friends. Maggie had been abandoned at an early age, and Eunice Mae had been ex-communicated by her own family when she broke away to join the war effort. But none of that mattered to the Baldwin family. Maggie and Eunice Mae alike had been fully and completely embraced as a lifelong member of the family.

"Well," said Dr. Forester, "I have very good news. Ms. Eunice is going to make a full recovery. She just had an attack of angina, the result of a little too much rich food yesterday, she admitted. She had been experimenting on some new dishes and sampled more than she realized. I take it she doesn't consume a very heavy diet on a regular basis."

Jessica almost giggled. What Dr. Forester described sounded just like something Eunice Mae would do. Color outside the lines. Push the speed limit. Climb a tree, if the urge should strike. The shear release of pent-up tension threatened to bust out of her in laughter. She reined in her emotions, however, forced her face to stay somber, and asked the most pressing question.

"Can we see her?" said Jessica, standing to her feet.

"Certainly. But give us about 30 minutes to move her to a room. We want to keep her overnight to make sure there are no surprises."

Jessica felt relief flood her soul. Ms. Eunice would live to see another day. She would be with them a while longer. *Thank You, Jesus.*

"Thank you," she said aloud, to the doctor. "We're very grateful for your help. God has brought Ms. Eunice through many adventures, and we're hoping she'll be with us for a good long time to come."

"Well, she seems very healthy," said Dr. Forester. "Like I said, give us a half hour. Someone will come tell you a room number shortly."

"Thanks again, Doctor," said Catherine.

"Happy endings are my favorite. You folks have a good day. If all goes well, Ms. Eunice will be out of here in time for lunch tomorrow. But nothing too rich for a few days," he said, as he turned to go.

106 ARROWHEAD DRIVE

Matthew Baldwin tried to relax. Again. Well aware that his jaw ached from clenching and unclenching, clenching and unclenching, he redirected his thoughts away from Jessica's assignment in Afghanistan. But only for a moment at a time. He'd heard about the nightmares that woke her in the middle of the night, and they triggered a few old memories of his own.

Thunder rattled the windows and rain fell in sheets. Matt had settled in at his desk to pen a letter to Jessica. She had already been back in Lubbock for several days, and he knew she must still be reeling from her experience in that hellish war zone—where, in his opinion, she never should have been in the first place. Although he knew she would be working on the story to meet a deadline, he had already called her a dozen times. He'd begun to hear a bit of irritation in her voice when she'd answer the phone, so he decided he'd go old school and send her a letter through snail mail. He vowed not to send it digitally. That he would refrain from calling her, and try to wait until he heard from her. But waiting would not be easy.

Matt sealed the envelope and affixed the stamp. He would drop it in the mail in the morning. Until then, he would occupy his time another way. He turned his attention to the *Time* magazine he had picked up at the airport that morning, and read the third article regarding the life of Eunice Mae Howell. When not delayed by some major world crisis, the articles had each been saved until the third publication of any given month, in order to give the feel of an ongoing adventure story.

Matt settled in to read every word at his leisure, and take the time to peruse the details of the myriad of photos that accompanied the article. Hopefully, it would take his mind off Afghanistan.

Article Three

Eunice Mae Howell met her husband while in training at Avenger Field in Sweetwater, Texas. I asked her to tell us how that came about.

"Well," said Eunice Mae, following a hearty laugh, "we ladies liked to keep a nice tan when we could. All of us being female, we were not shy about sunbathing in our underwear, sometimes even from the cockpit." Eunice Mae chuckled again.

"Once we arrived at Avenger Field, the male trainees at surrounding stations began flying over our quarters. They would call in a distress signal, like an engine running rough, or some such thing, when their aircraft had no real need of repair. Then they got word, I guess, that some of us would sunbathe from the cockpit. You can imagine what a stir that created. I'm pretty sure the practice ended when one of us, who shall remain nameless, had been sunbathing while flying, and suddenly found herself flanked on both sides by two male pilots. When she grabbed for her shirt, the wind sucked it right out of the open cockpit. She immediately returned to base and asked her bunk mate to run inside and get a blanket to wrap around her, before she would get out of the plane. We made good times out of bad whenever we could.

"But back to your question. My husband, William Masters Howell, had called in a rough running engine and landed at Avenger Field. As fate would have it, I happened to be walking out from my bunk as he descended from his plane. I had just showered and put on a halter top and shorts. He had removed his helmet. So he saw me, and I saw him, and there was eye contact, and a smile, and a wave. After training, he went his way, and I went mine. But it wasn't the last I would see of Bill Howell.

"I received a letter every week from him until."

Eunice Mae reached for the hanky she kept in her shirt pocket, wiped a tear then continued with her story.

"Until he became a prisoner of war. I won't get into the gory details of that nightmare. But Bill survived and made his way back home, a mere two days after Japan surrendered."

I asked Eunice Mae where home had been for Bill Howell.

"Bill grew up in Atlanta, Georgia. It took several months for him to recover physically from his ordeal as a prisoner of war, and much longer to heal emotionally. Anyway, he contacted the War Department to find out where I had ended up, and the letters started coming again. Once I finished my duty with WASP, I made an attempt to return to Savannah. But there seemed to be no point by then. Both of my parents had passed away, and the family blamed me for not being around.

"So, I took care of business, and set out to find a career suitable for someone with my experience."

Eunice Mae applied to be a pilot with a commercial airline, and hired on as a co-pilot. Within two years, she had been promoted to Captain.

"Even today," says Eunice Mae, "only 5% of commercial pilots are female. And back in my day men weren't too excited to fly with a woman, even an experienced flyer. Many of the men I came into contact with didn't like the new way. Under the old society, men ruled in every aspect of life. They liked knowing 'the little woman' was at home, saddled with two or three kids, living on his appointed budget, and taking the kids to church on Sunday, whether he went or not. It made most of those men feel important and needed, and if he got lucky, appreciated.

"When men like that were forced to work with someone like me, someone fiercely independent, with a husband who backed me, and no children who needed me to nurture them, it made some male pilots, and even some male passengers, uncomfortable. I remember this one passenger who had been going to a therapist trying to get over his fear of flying. When he saw me in the cockpit, he about came undone. He said his therapist told him that if anything about a particular aircraft made him uncomfortable, he should skip that flight and take the next available one. 'And I'm just not comfortable putting my life in the hands of a woman,' he told me.

"I wanted to laugh, but figured that would be rude. So, I told him I was not offended, and wanted him to do whatever made him comfortable. He disembarked without another word, and I never saw him again.

"But I didn't stop flying. And that was really the most extreme case of prejudice I ever encountered. Then, once I made Captain, I never had another minute of trouble with male co-pilots. And I flew for 30 years. All-in-all, a great career, for a female with no family."

I asked again about her husband.

"Oh yes," she said. "Bill and I married five years after he got out of the service. He joined me here in Lubbock. By then, I had had the family home in Savannah disassembled, and reassembled here. He lived twenty years, and then died of lung cancer. He never could shake the cigarette habit he acquired during the war. We weren't able to have children, and Bill was very accepting of my career. He flew everywhere I did, and we had a great time."

I asked Eunice Mae if she would advise against a flying career for a woman with a husband and children.

"I would never tell a woman not to do something her heart desired to do. That would be ludicrous. Her life is her life, and she should make the call. But being a pilot requires a lot of expensive training, unless you train in the military, like I did. But even then the continuing education requirements are quite taxing. You're gone from home a lot, and the hours are nowhere near a nine-to-five job. I would advise a young lady to examine all the requirements and possibilities, in advance.

"Pilot jobs are scarcer now than they used to be, too. I read recently about an aspiring female pilot who wanted to work for a commercial airline, but no jobs were available. So, her first two years as a pilot she flew for Fed Ex. Not a bad way to get some flight hours and experience, to my way of thinking."

So, there you have it, ladies. If you're looking for a viable and rewarding career, follow your heart and do your research. And one day, you might find yourself looking back and enjoying with satisfaction a wealth of great memories, and knowing you lived life to the fullest.

Stay tuned for more in the life of Eunice Mae Howell.

Chapter 13

With God we will gain the victory, and he will trample down our enemies
(Psalm 108:13 NIV).

AS MATT closed the magazine, more enamored than ever with both Jessica and Ms. Eunice, his cell phone vibrated on the walnut coffee table in front of the loveseat, where he had begun to read.

He grinned when he saw JESS displayed across the screen. Maybe she didn't need a letter to remind herself to call him, after all. His smile faded, however, when he heard the stress in her voice. Even though they were separated by nearly 350 miles, it seemed he could feel the vibrations that traveled through the air, could feel the ache that penetrated her soul.

"Jess, what is it? What's happened?"

"The news is good, Matt. Really. It's just been a long day. Ms. Eunice had a scare. We thought she was having a heart attack. Turned out to be a simple case of angina. She's fine, and saucy as ever. We'll be taking her home in the morning. I waited to call until I could be positive about what to say. She really is doing well."

Matt let out a breath. *Thank You, Lord. What a tragedy it would be to lose Ms. Eunice at this juncture. Thanks for letting us enjoy her a while longer.*

"So, the doctor didn't find anything alarming?" he said aloud.

"No. Said he hoped to be half the man at her age."

"That is good news. And how are you?"

"Better. I finished the Afghanistan story and submitted it just before Eunice Mae had to go to the hospital. Which I'm very grateful for. It would have taken a lot for me to get back into it."

"And how are you doing at night?"

"What?"

"Marilyn talked to Mother."

"Oh."

"Can I help?"

"You can pray for me. I'll get through this. The peace of God is my only hope; so prayer would be greatly appreciated."

"Consider it done. I'm relieved to hear that Ms. Eunice will soon be herself again. And I will earnestly be praying for a full measure of peace for you."

Even though Jessica had called him the day before, Matt dropped the letter he'd written to her in the mail the following morning, as planned. It contained words he had not said to her in person. He couldn't be sure she was ready to hear them. Couldn't be sure if she felt the same way. When he laid his head down to sleep, his prayers turned immediately for peace to soothe her wounded soul, for the healing power of Jesus Christ to heal the wounds caused by trauma, caused by the sights and sounds she had endured over there. And prayed further that Jessica would more closely examine the assignments offered her—before she got maimed or killed. The thought of losing her had become unbearable, even though they had made no long-term commitment. Even though he had not asked her to be his own. The time she had spent in Afghanistan had unnerved him. The delay in her return had scared him. The sight of her at the airport, alive and whole, and a little too thin, had convinced him that he needed her in his life. Would always need her.

One Week Later

Jessica rang the doorbell at Eunice Mae's house at nine in the morning, hoping she would not be too early. She hadn't taken the time to call, afraid she would talk herself out of coming. Her heart was heavy; but she didn't want to talk to her mother, or even Kim. She wanted Ms. Eunice's opinion. A woman who had been independent all of her life, experienced many exciting adventures, and had managed to work love into the formula. Jessica needed to know how she did that. If she would do it that way all over again, if given the chance. She wanted to know if Ms. Eunice's independence had cost her something she wished she had never given up.

With one foot tapping to an imaginary song, Jessica waited at Eunice Mae's door. Under her arm, Jessica carried the latest *Time* magazine with Ms. Eunice's picture on the cover. Jessica had received Matt's letter in the mail two days ago, and had it tucked away inside the magazine.

Jessica wanted to go over the latest article with Ms. Eunice, yes. But today, she was using it as an excuse to have a long chat about romance. An intimate conversation with a passionate woman, who had loved passionately, while still holding on to her independence and self-worth. Jessica had to know how Eunice Mae had made it work.

Before long, Eunice Mae opened the door and stared openly at Jessica.

"What's the matter? Is my face green?" said Jessica.

"No," said Eunice Mae, drawing out the "o" in her delightful southern accent. "It's covered in tears."

"Oh, that," said Jessica. "Could we talk?"

Tears. She shouldn't be surprised. Jessica had just been crying all morning, and apparently didn't notice now, when she was crying and when she was not. She had dropped yesterday's mail on the table by the door and not thought about it until later in the evening. She'd had the task of unpacking the last of the boxes on her mind, so didn't even read Matt's letter until she settled on the bed with her back propped against a pillow. The depth of feeling he portrayed in the letter both thrilled and frightened her. She loved Matt Baldwin; she knew that. But this letter hinted at marriage. Was she ready for that? She still had a lot of traveling and writing and photo-shooting to do. Could she have a rewarding career that took her all over the world, and be a loving and devoted wife at the same time? Would Matt be willing to settle for a wife who might not be home every night to put supper on the table? Would he eradicate the need for freedom and adventure that coursed through her veins? Could she love him enough to give up her career to play it safe? Would she wind up hurting both of them?

The questions had roared through her mind half the night. Ms. Eunice seemed to be the only solution. A warm, gentle woman who cared about her, understood her, and also had tackled life head-on, just the way Jessica planned to.

"Yes, my dear, of course," Jessica heard Ms. Eunice say. "Come in out of the damp. Since this cold front hit, I've been chilled to the bone. I was just making a fresh pot of coffee. And I have a surprise for you. You do like lattes, right?"

"I've learned to, since I met you," said Jessica, as she wiped tears with the back of her hands. She stepped inside, and shrugged out of her jacket. "Thank you, Ms. Eunice. Sorry I didn't call. I wanted to show you the new article and chat awhile, if you have the time. Thought we might check it out together."

"I'd be delighted to have your company, and see the new article. And don't worry about not calling. Far as I'm concerned, this is your home, too. Let's do the article first and get it over with. I want to spend all the time we need on the real reason you came over. Well, you know where the coat rack is. I'll meet you at the breakfast bar in a moment."

Jessica settled at the breakfast bar, closed her eyes, and sighed, her head rested on her left hand, as though she could not hold it up on its own. She watched Eunice Mae intently, noticing for the first time, really, that Ms. Eunice seemed to be moving slower than usual. As she watched Eunice Mae struggle with the tea kettle filled with hot water, Jessica hopped down off the stool and scooted around the end of the breakfast bar.

"Here, let me help, Ms. Eunice."

"Thank you. That pot didn't seem so heavy yesterday."

Jessica fought back the frown that would have expressed her ever-growing concern. Could this really be happening? The same charismatic, sharp, sturdy lady of a mere three months ago had suddenly aged. Seemingly, overnight. Or maybe Eunice Mae was just having an off day. Surely, God wasn't through with her on Earth. Jessica wasn't, anyway, and committed in that moment to pray for Eunice Mae's strength and vitality for as long as she remained on the planet.

Jessica poured two mugs of mocha lattes while Eunice Mae arranged a platter of key lime cooler cookies, like the ones made famous in Savannah, Georgia. Jessica could not resist them—and Eunice Mae knew it.

"Yum, my favorite," said Jessica.

"They've been a weakness of mine for more years than I'd care to count," said Eunice Mae. "Now, come sit with me in the den, and we'll get this article business out of the way."

Jessica sighed with relief. At least Eunice Mae *sounded* like herself. Physical weakness did not necessarily indicate mental feebleness.

The two of them got comfortable on the burgundy leather sofa in the den, with the plate of cookies on the coffee table in front of them, and began their review of the fourth article.

Article Four

Let me tell you more about this amazing woman. Eunice Mae Howell did not hang up her helmet when they closed the WASP program. She became a commercial pilot, like I said before. Neither did she sit on a couch and knit booties for other people's grandchildren after retirement. Eunice Mae stayed active. She joined a local gym, jogged two and three miles before breakfast, and kept her mind sharp by taking a different course at Texas Tech University every semester, in one subject or another. She holds three Masters degrees, and didn't retire from being a part-time student until her 85th birthday!

Let me tell you about an adventure Eunice Mae participated in right here in Lubbock County, several years ago. A bully had been picking on her closest friend's family and had been hired to burn down their house! Eunice Mae literally took matters into her own hands, and the perpetrator was brought to justice. Below is an abbreviated rendition of that adventure:

Over a light supper of chef salad, peppermint tea and pineapple sherbet, Eunice Mae, her good friend, Maggie, and Maggie's employer, Catherine Baldwin, discussed a possible course of action. Such a bold move would require discretion, stealth and cunning. They needed someone on the inside to "spy" on Elizabeth Baldwin, the alleged villain, the person who had hired a punk named Joe to burn down her own son's deserted estate—simply to keep her daughter-in-law from being able to later claim anything she might have left behind.

A member in good standing of the local "upper crust," Eunice Mae offered to conduct an investigation of her own. She would be the closest thing they might find to "someone on the inside."

"This is going to be great fun," said Eunice Mae, rubbing her hands together with glee. "Mrs. Baldwin is way overdue for her comeuppance. And if anyone can get to her, it's me. Far as I know, I'm the only one she's ever invited to stay over for dinner after Tuesday bridge club. I don't know why really, except I pretty much let her do the talking. She seems to like the sound of her own voice.

"She does have a soft spot, though. I've seen her get disgustingly sentimental after a few martinis. Just tell me what you want to know, and I'll do the best I can to deliver the information in a timely manner."

A glint in her eye betrayed the bold, feisty Eunice Mae of her youth.

"I'll share my story with you, Eunice Mae, but only if you promise not to do anything too risky or stupid," said Catherine Baldwin. "No victory would be worth the price of hurting a friend."

"She means what she says," said Maggie. "At the moment, we have nothing to lose; but if you get on Elizabeth Baldwin's hit list, you could lose everything."

"Don't worry about me. I can battle that old buzzard, dollar for dollar. I'll be fine."

"Promise me you'll back off if your plan goes sour," said Catherine.

"I can see you're serious, and I respect that," said Eunice Mae, sobering. "I promise to be careful."

"Good enough," said Catherine.

"I'll trust you, too," said Maggie. "I know you're a woman of your word."

And so it began.

Maggie adjusted the sunshades on her nose and peeked out over the newspaper to make sure Eunice Mae wasn't walking into a booby trap. Eunice Mae had worked up the nerve to buy a shotgun in the "black market".

"Illegal is what I call it," said Maggie.

But Eunice Mae wasn't about to put her well-known name on a firearms registration form; and Maggie didn't want to be seen anywhere near what she called an armory. So the black market it was. Eunice Mae would never disclose where she got her information, which was just as well, because Maggie didn't want the responsibility of knowing such a thing.

The sun was near setting, already sunken to a dark orange. The last rays of a tense evening that Maggie sorely wanted to see come to an end. She breathed a sigh of relief as Eunice Mae came around the corner from the alley, carrying a four-foot Christmas tree box. The espionage had begun.

Maggie didn't exactly know how she should feel, exhilarated or terrified. She and Eunice Mae were about to embark on the adventure of a lifetime, that could cost them their lives.

Without consulting another living soul, Eunice Mae and Maggie had decided to follow this character around who had been hired by Elizabeth Baldwin. Follow him—of all the crazy things for a couple of old ladies to do—especially since they had not breathed a word of their plan to anyone who might be able to come to the rescue.

Planning ahead, Eunice Mae had thought to give the maid and driver the day off. She had counted the hours and minutes until time to execute her plan. Adrenalin pumped the blood faster through her veins, and she felt young again. Life took on new meaning and purpose. An injustice was about to be done, and she was determined to stop it.

"What do you think, Maggie? Are you ready?"

"I could never be ready for such a crazy stunt, and I can't believe you actually intend to go through with it. I would rather call the police and leave it in their hands. We're two old ladies who have no business getting ourselves killed for no good reason."

"No good reason!" cried Eunice Mae. "This is your family we're talking about, Maggie. Do you want their homestead destroyed, their legacy erased, all memory of their father buried in the rubble?"

"What kind of a question is that? Of course not."

"Then let's go stop Joe Maxwell before it's too late."

"Well, I'm certainly not going to let you go off and get killed by yourself. Maybe your information was wrong, and the guy won't show up at all."

"Maybe, but I'm not taking that chance. I'm going."

Maggie rolled her eyes, but held her tongue and helped Eunice Mae clear off the table and load the rented van.

Maggie pulled their spy mobile into the driveway of a vacant lot across the alley from the Baldwin mansion, and altogether missed Eunice Mae's Cadillac. Catherine had borrowed it for the morning, and parked it two houses to the north. Maggie had tried, to no avail, to persuade Eunice Mae to abandon this silly notion of catching the bad guy on her own. She couldn't think of the right thing to do in order to stop her, and even found herself helping unload an extra box of shells (in case of a shoot-out), the four-foot Christmas tree box that concealed Eunice Mae's black-market shotgun, and a carefully packed picnic basket, just in case a long vigil proved necessary.

In all the mystery surrounding the hiring of Joe Maxwell, he managed to avoid being charged with what he was about to do. Elizabeth Baldwin did not confess, and Joe Maxwell did not implicate her. He simply had "approached the wrong address for an electrical repair job he had been hired to do." Never mind that no one in the neighborhood could remember having hired anyone to do any electrical repair for more than six months prior.

Kimberly disappeared, almost immediately following the incident. The ransom call came in just 24 hours after Joe Maxwell's release.

Eunice Mae signaled to Maggie, waving her into the kitchen.

"I knew it had to be him," said Eunice Mae. "He's just that brazen. He should have taken Elizabeth's down payment and run, when he had the chance. Look Maggie, we know where this guy lives. And we know he is guilty. What if he stashed our little Kim right there in his house? Let's go find out."

Just the thought that they might be able to rescue Kim had Eunice Mae's blood stirred up again.

"No," stated Maggie, her hands planted firmly on her hips, defiance in her eyes. "Emphatically, no."

"Don't you see?" said Eunice Mae. "If we're right, we will save the day. And if we're wrong, we will have eliminated one of Joe's probable hideouts. Kidnapping is a major crime. He won't walk away from a kidnapping charge. Come on, Maggie. Humor me."

Once again, Maggie and Eunice Mae set out to trap Joe Maxwell, to catch him in the act, and make sure he paid for his crimes. No one messes with the family and friends of Eunice Mae Howell, and gets away with it, without a fight.

"Here we are," said Eunice Mae. "Roll very slowly up the alley and park where you can see the back gate. But not too close for detection."

Maggie complied.

Eunice Mae took in her friend's profile. Both hands still gripped the steering wheel. A crease drew her brows together in a frown. Her skin glowed with nervous perspiration.

"Don't be afraid, Maggie. Nothing bad is going to happen to Kim. I promise. If I'm right, I'll call the FBI immediately. And you can call the Ransom Canyon Police Department."

"Let's call them now," said Maggie.

"And tell them what?"

"Just relax and wait, Mags. It's only a few hours before the scheduled drop. Joe has to leave Kim somewhere while he goes after the money."

Five minutes later:

"Eunice Mae. Hurry!" cried Maggie.

Eunice Mae came barreling through the front gate, running toward Maggie. She took in a big gulp of air before she spoke.

"My stars, Maggie. What's wrong? Are you hurt?"

"No," said Maggie, her voice dropping to a whisper as she held her hand up to shush her friend. "Listen. I think I hear someone inside the tool shed."

"Well, great honk, girl. Let's go see."

Eunice Mae stomped off toward the tool shed, confident in her stance, bold in her demeanor. Once she reached the small building, she noticed a pad lock on the door.

"Drat," she spat. "Maggie. Go out front and fetch one of those policemen. I don't know who alerted them, but I saw a squad car parked in front of the house. Tell him we need a pad lock cut off. Now scoot."

It was a proud day for the Ransom Canyon Police Department. Kim Baldwin, rescued by the day shift. They would certainly make the headlines for this feat. As soon as Kimberly Anne Baldwin emerged from the tool shed, the newest part-time officer took off toward the patrol car to radio the FBI.

"We've found her, sir," he announced. "Yes, sir, I'm sure. We've found Kimberly Baldwin. Yes, sir. She is most definitely alive. The psycho left her in the tool shed, right here in the back yard of the Baldwin Estate. Yes, sir. An ambulance is on the way. I'll radio back as soon as I know which hospital."

The two men in the purple van out front sat on the curb with their hands cuffed behind their backs, frightened half out of their wits. They had nearly been arrested for kidnapping, and would have to wait it out until the commotion out back died down, and wonder what was to become of them for digging a hole for a tree—in the wrong front yard. Erroneously captured because a nosey neighbor made an anonymous phone call.

So there you have it, folks. Eunice Mae Howell has been a hero since her teenage years. This journalist has been blessed to spend a few invigorating weeks getting to know her better. So, I urge you, female or otherwise, to follow your dreams. Don't sit on the sidelines and let the world pass you by. Stand up for what you believe. Love those whom God has placed in your lives. Treasure the friends you make along the way. And be bold. Be strong. Be courageous.

Stay tuned for one last article in celebration of all those brave souls who served with WASP. We salute you.

Chapter 14

The Lord has heard my cry for mercy; the Lord accepts my prayer
(Psalm 6:9 NIV).

JESSICA lingered on Eunice Mae's sofa, staring at nothing in particular, hesitant to bring up the real reason she had sought Ms. Eunice's company. She felt keenly aware of the cold, damp, dreary day, for it mirrored her mood. She didn't know where to go from here. How to proceed with her relationship with a certain could-this-guy-be-for-real commercial pilot who had captured her heart, and over the past few days, a great deal of her thoughts. Jessica couldn't get him out of her head. But she came around at the sound of Eunice Mae's voice.

"What is the true reason you came to see me, Jessica? I can tell you have something weighing on you."

Her voice was soft, filled with compassion. Eunice Mae did not elaborate on the article they had just read that heralded her as a hero. Her heart remained focused on her friend. Jessica admired Eunice Mae more than any woman she had ever known. Oh, she loved her mother, and the women in Kim's family, for sure. Brave women who had endured much, embraced the love and grace of Christ, and stood strong in the face of much adversity. She loved them all, but honestly, they seemed rather ordinary compared with Eunice Mae Howell. Jessica longed to live the life of adventure Ms. Eunice had lived. Jessica considered Eunice Mae a hero. Her hero.

Jessica looked over at Eunice Mae. "It's true. I admit it. I came to find out how you managed to live such a full life and still give your heart to a man. Were you ever sorry you married?"

"Oh, so that's it. Has Matt proposed?"

"No, but I think it's coming."

Without another word, Jessica handed Ms. Eunice the letter she had received from Matt.

"Are you sure you want me to read this? Are you sure Matt would be okay with it?"

"Yes, and I don't know. But I need your advice. I won't tell him I let you read it, if you won't tell him."

"Okay," said Eunice Mae. "I understand. It will be our secret."

Eunice Mae opened the letter with great care. A knowing deep in her soul stirred her heart. Of all the adventures of her life, her relationship with Bill Howell had been one of the greatest, sweetest, most treasured memories contained in her journals. Part of her felt a surge of excitement, for she knew God had granted her a front-row seat in the lives of two wonderful young people who belonged to Him—and in Eunice Mae's estimation, belonged together.

She closed her eyes and breathed in a prayer for wisdom and thanksgiving. Wisdom for the right words to share with Jessica, and thanksgiving that God had brought the three of them together, and that He trusted Eunice Mae to be obedient. Eunice Mae refocused her attention on the task at hand and began to read the letter Matt had penned to Jessica.

Jess, I feel a little silly using snail mail to send you a letter. However, since I had become a pest following your return from Afghanistan, I thought it best to put a little distance between my words and your ears. And there are things I wish to say that you may need to ponder before you respond.

I spent many a fitful night while you were away on assignment, praying for your safety, pleading with God to send angels, extra big warrior angels, to watch over you. Maggie would have fussed at me. "Why bother to pray if you're gonna worry? Worry and doubt keep angels from fulfilling the assignment you asked to send them on in the first place." I had to remind myself of that every day when I prayed. I believe God honored my faith, sent the angels to rescue you, and they saw to it you were returned safely to us. And I'm extremely grateful.

Anyway, back to the point of this letter. I can't think of anything original and clever, so I'll just stick to the oldies, but goodies. Here are a few: "I've never met a girl like you before." "I was smitten, the minute I laid eyes on you." "You're the most beautiful woman I've ever seen."

I'll dispense with any more of that. It just goes downhill from there. I do admire you a great deal, I want you to know. More than I've ever thought I'd feel for any woman. I think about you throughout the day and dream of you at night. I miss you when we're not together and struggle when we have to be apart. In the short time I have known you, Jess, I have grown to love you. My prayer is that you will one day love me, too. Love me enough to marry me. Love me enough to become one with me. Love me enough to raise a family with me.

I'd like to say a lot more in that regard, but will wait until I know if my feelings are reciprocated. I'm proud of you, both as an individual and as a journalist. You may be a little too good at your job. Ha! But elaborating on that can wait, as well.

I pray you are recovering rapidly from your ordeal. Please know that I am only a phone call away. I'll go now, until there is a convenient time for us to speak face-to-face.

Forever yours, Matt

Ms. Eunice re-folded the letter and put it back inside the envelope with a grin.

"Sounds like he loves you, all right. Do you love him?"

"Of course I do. That's the problem."

"Really. How so?"

"To be completely honest, I've been afraid I might lose my independence, have to give up traveling, and be forced to take safe assignments close to home."

"Did Matthew say that?"

Eunice Mae had read only a hint of such things in Matt's letter, and felt sure he would never make demands on Jessica. She thought she knew him better than that after the years she'd spent listening to Maggie talk about him, brag on him, and miss him so much it hurt, once he left home. And from what she'd learned secretly communicating with him while he served in the Navy, as well as the sweet things she'd heard about him since his return, she believed he had matured, grown into a precious man of God. No, she could not fathom a man of Matt's caliber deliberately stifling Jessica in her career choices. Or in any way, for that matter.

But Jessica would have to discover all those wonderful traits for herself. Few people in the family understood a need for adventure like Matthew. According to Maggie, he had been fearless from toddlerhood. Maggie had loved Matt a great deal, and had often come to Eunice Mae for advice—being the only other person she knew who acted anything like Matthew Baldwin. Eunice Mae understood the call of the wild, like few women of her generation.

Matt might be concerned for Jessica's safety; what decent man wouldn't be? Eunice Mae remembered how distraught Matthew had been when Jessica had been kidnapped, gone on assignment to Israel, and again when she'd been trapped in a war zone in Afghanistan. But neither she nor Jessica would ever know for sure until they talked to Matthew about it directly—and he wasn't in the room at the moment.

"No," said Jessica, "he didn't say anything *exactly*, except that he wants to marry me someday. It seems to me, that one act alone would come with a lot of restrictions. How did you manage, Ms. Eunice? You had a husband and a career, and I know you were fiercely independent."

Eunice Mae laughed. "Still am. But a thing like that can be carried to extremes. I was a little too independent, if you know what I mean."

"No, ma'am, I don't. I think I would have loved being you, living your life—one big adventure after another."

Eunice Mae didn't speak for a long time. She didn't want to discourage Jessica's adventurous spirit. How could she? But at the same time, she didn't want her response to push Jessica away from romance—a big adventure in its own right. And Eunice Mae didn't want Jessica to one day be in the position to have to be adopted into a family because she had been estranged from her own. How different might her life have been if Eunice Mae had yielded a little? Been a little less independent. Even a little give, may have made a major difference. But it was too late for speculation. Even so, her experience might help this young girl. Isn't that what experience was for? To pass on acquired wisdom to others in need of it? Of course, for it to help, the recipient of such wisdom would need to heed the advice and act on it. Naturally.

Eunice Mae inhaled, set her mug on the alabaster coaster in front of her then turned to face Jessica.

"My dear," she began, with caution. "True love doesn't come with chains. Godly love comes with freedom. Yes, concessions must be made for another human being when a marriage takes place. Sometimes family has to come first. But I believe any sacrifice you might be called upon to make for the sake of a loved one would prove to be well worth the effort."

"Really?"

"Yes, really. Can you even imagine life without your mother, your best friend, or her family? Without girlfriends or colleagues, or co-workers?"

Eunice Mae watched with interest as Jessica's facial expression changed, then smiled with relief at Jessica's answer. Hope lit up Eunice Mae's eyes. This young woman would one day figure out the correct order for her priorities. Yes, there was hope.

"Honestly, no," said Jessica.

"Well, I can. And at times it was most unpleasant. I lived that way for many years, Jessica. Many lonely years, until the Lord smiled on me, and introduced me to Maggie. Without God and the Baldwin family, I would still be desperately alone. Independent or not, estranged from one's family is a sad way to live, especially in the throes of widowhood. Added to that, there had been no children in my life. No one left to love me when my family turned a deaf ear to me, when my extended family rejected me because my parents passed away while I was serving in WASP. No son or daughter to laugh and cry with when life brought sorrow or victory. No one, Jessica. Simply no one. Without God's love and abiding presence, I'm sure I would have gone quite mad.

"Look, sweetie," Eunice Mae continued, as she patted Jessica's hand. "Promise me you won't make such an important decision before you talk to God about it. Before you see Matt face-to-face and discuss your feelings. Don't let love slip away because of the poor example my life has been. If I had been less stubborn, I would have been there to tell my mother, and then my father, goodbye, before they departed this life. If I had taken leave to go home, taken time away from my own selfish ambition, I would have felt their arms about me once again, heard their voices, and seen love in their eyes.

"Promise me you will pray, child."

Jessica's assignment in Afghanistan had triggered a few memories for Matt, as well. Several nights in a row, he woke in a panic, thinking he'd crashed in the middle of a war zone. Again. The flash of memories, body parts, blood, children dead in the streets, buildings collapsing and car bombs wreaking havoc, filled his dreams. Friends' faces with dull, dead eyes, limbs missing from his best buddy, and then watching him bleed out before the medic could get to him. The suffocating heat and cold nights. He'd been home nearly a year now, and thought the dreams a thing of the past. Not so.

He would climb out of bed, dripping with sweat, and make his way to the living room, turning on every light along the way, as his lounge chair called his name. He would lean back, careful to keep his eyes open, then reach for his Bible. The sweet peace of Jesus had been his salvation when he'd first come back from deployment. It would be again.

But it took a solid week of turmoil for Matt to feel somewhat normal again. The week had made him wonder about the details of Jessica's dreams. A realist, she would show all and tell all in the article. He didn't much look forward to reading it. Memories had been stirred just hearing the name, Afghanistan. Would he be able to handle pictures, revealing phrases that would conjure up his own set of traumatic recollections, just when he felt he'd gotten a handle on them? Maybe, in support of Jessica's efforts. Then again, maybe not. He would have to wait and see.

The time had come for him to revisit the past, to be healed in the tender parts of his heart and mind that he had avoided with great care. Matt dropped to his knees beside his chair and cried out to Jesus. In that moment, Matt realized he still had wounds deep in his soul. Wounds no one else could see. Wounds he had pushed aside and tried to ignore. He had managed to gain control of his faculties, presented a calm and confident demeanor to the world, and had fooled even himself—for a while. But now, as he prayed for the blood of Jesus to cover any unconfessed sin, it came to him that he had not forgiven himself for being offended by the enemy, and had not forgiven the enemy for killing his friend.

A prayer came to mind that he had jotted down while watching Katie Souza on YouTube. For months, he had been meaning to look her up, after a pilot friend told him about her. God's timing worked in his favor, for the prayer Katie introduced him to was fresh on his mind. He had memorized it the day before. He might not remember it word-for-word, but he intended to try. A prayer of healing from trauma. A timely prayer he believed could serve as his deliverance from the ravages of war. Finally.

Matt began in a whisper.

"Dear Lord, wash me clean of any sin involved in my trauma. I repent for anything I've done that was considered sin. I take responsibility for any part of the trauma that was my fault. I ask that You would wash me clean of all sin. I believe, as I am repenting, I'm being forgiven of every sin that I took part in during this horrible event. I sincerely forgive anyone who was associated with my trauma, no matter what they did. I forgive them because I'm getting healed, right now, of the wounds in my soul that came from that trauma. So, I forgive them and I repent for holding unforgiveness in my heart."

Matt raised his voice a notch.

"In the name of Jesus, I command the same power that raised Christ from the dead to be released in my soul. I decree the power is flooding my soul as I reach out to touch the hem of Your garment. The power is going back to the trauma and healing me at the root.

I command the healing power of the resurrection to remove every picture that is burned into my mind that came from that horrible situation. I command the power to heal every painful emotion that is connected with the horrors of the war in Afghanistan. I command any lingering wound in my soul or in my body to be miraculously healed. I command complete physical and emotional restoration to happen now, in Jesus' name, that I may become the meaning of dunamis, the power that raised Christ from the dead, the power to perform miracles, and be excellent of soul."

In a very short time, Matt had come to love that phrase: "excellent of soul." The phrase alone conjured up a beautiful picture. Perhaps the best a human soul could be, while still bound to this earth. Excellent.

For a solid hour, Matt remained immersed in the healing light of Jesus Christ. He moved to kneel in front of his chair, head in hands. Then after a time, he shifted from his knees to lying prostrate at his Father's feet, until the healing power of the resurrection flooded him, filled his heart, his mind, his soul, his entire body.

When Matt opened his eyes, he did not know the time, did not realize the hour, for it seemed as though his prayer had only lasted a few minutes. But the effects of the prayer showed visible signs that the work of the light had carried on for the entire time he had been engaged in prayer. He lifted his left arm far above his head, and knew his rotator cuff injury had been completely healed. Miraculously healed. He examined his heart and realized he no longer felt murderous malice toward the Muslim community—not even the violent sect that had started this war.

God had healed him, emotionally and physically. The prayers he would pray in the future regarding a lost and dying culture would be that someone, somewhere, somehow, would reach past the blind hatred and convince them, one man at a time, one soul at a time, that Jesus really is the Truth, the Way and the Life.

Matt stood to his feet, stretched, shouted, danced a jig, and praised the Lord, grateful for freedom in Christ; grateful for the love that still glowed warm in his heart.

He returned to bed, overjoyed and exhausted at the same time, knowing he would sleep good—extra good. Knowing his life would never be the same again.

Early Friday morning, Matt donned his uniform, checked his reflection in the mirror, and noticed a light in his eyes that had been gone for as long as he could remember. Hadn't even registered, till now. He hadn't realized how dark his soul had remained, following his participation in the war. Once again, just in case, he re-examined his heart.

"Thank You, Lord. The malice is totally gone! Only the power of God could accomplish such a feat."

Surely, the realization that we need to plead the blood of Jesus to forgive ourselves and others, coupled with the awesomeness of the resurrection power to heal physical and mental issues alike, would catch on. We need all of who Jesus is—the blood shed on the cross and the power of the resurrection! Of course we do!

Matt felt like a new man, and wanted very much to share this treasure with Jessica. The thought of her brought up the letter he had mailed now more than a week ago. She had not answered—by snail mail, text, e-mail, or any other way. No matter. He had shared his heart in a physical, on paper, in his own handwriting, letter. How romantic is that? It had to mean something to her. Had to trigger some level of emotion.

Even so, he could wait. Jessica had a lot to think about right now—without throwing a marriage proposal into the mix. God's timing for them would prove to be perfect. He would believe, for as long as Jessica would allow it, that they were meant to be together.

Matt backed out of the driveway with a smile on his face. He would have a two-hour layover in Lubbock today, and Jessica had agreed to meet him at the airport.

Jessica waited at the bottom of the escalator, eager to see Matt's face as he rounded the corner at the top of the stairs. It seemed like ages since she'd seen him, although it had only been a few weeks.

She froze when she spotted him. No man she had ever known could compare. A smile spread across his face as they made eye contact, and Jessica's heart skipped a beat.

"Good grief, he's gorgeous," she mumbled, as she watched him descend. She could not look away, nor did she desire to.

"Hello, gorgeous. Long time no see."

"Hello yourself. What did you want to do for two hours?"

"Nothing. Just be with you."

Relief flooded over Jessica. Matt had not started in on her with a demand for an answer to his letter. Although if he had, she would have said yes. Yes, yes, a thousand times, yes. She couldn't look in those eyes, and say anything else. The words Ms. Eunice had shared with her made it possible to entertain the idea of a life spent with Matthew Baldwin, a life of adventure *and* romance.

"That's lovely," said Jessica, retaining control of her emotions and her facial expression. The slightest deviation would give her away, and she needed a little more time. Just a little more time, and a lot more prayer. "How about a trip to a Sonic drive-in?"

"Sounds great. I could use a cherry lime-aid."

"Perfect. I'm not parked very far out."

Jessica could feel her heart pounding. Just walking beside Matt enlarged her ego. He did have flaws, didn't he? He had to. Everyone does. He is, after all, a human being.

Don't dwell on that, silly. There will be plenty of time for such discoveries later. For right now, enjoy today. You already know he loves you. Just don't wait too long, and give him a reason to look elsewhere.

Matthew would only be able to give her an hour, what with the time it takes to disembark, travel to Sonic and back, and prepare to board the plane in time to get ready for the next flight out.

Jessica felt a bit overwhelmed, and for a minute couldn't find her voice, or think of a single intelligent thing to say. Therefore, the walk to the car had been made in silence. A sigh of relief escaped her lips as she climbed in on the driver's side and waited for Matt to take a seat on the passenger's side. At least she would have something to focus on besides Matt Baldwin. Surely she could drive without losing her grip on reality.

Jessica pulled into the Sonic on 34th Street, hoping she had made the right choice. She couldn't be sure if she had saved time or cost them precious moments of what little time they had together. They could just as well have had a Coke at the airport. But no, that wouldn't do. She needed some privacy. Privacy afforded at a drive-in. A place where you were served in your car.

"What size lime-aid would you like?" said Jessica.

"I think just a medium. Don't want to have to leave the cockpit too often during a flight."

"Of course."

Jessica still felt nervous, and ordered a route 44 cranberry water, plus an ice cream cone. Comfort food wasn't named comfort food for no good reason.

"Would you like one?" she said.

"No, thank you. I usually make a mess with those things."

"Ok."

"Jess, you all right? You seem upset. It's just me sitting here, you know. I saw no sign of anyone tailing us. Did you?

Jessica released an odd-sounding chuckle, and made herself make eye contact with him.

He raised a brow, and watched with interest as her countenance fell.

"Did you have a hard time when you came back from Afghanistan?" she said.

So, that was the issue. Jessica needed a sounding board. Matt had come thinking they would talk about the letter. But he understood she must deal with this Afghanistan issue first. He could well identify with her present state of mind.

The feelings he had expressed in the letter would stand for all time; Jessica's emotional healing deserved the highest priority. But with just an hour to spare, how could he possibly make a difference? How could he explain his own nightmares, his own struggles? And he sure couldn't cover wounded souls and the light of Christ in such an abbreviated time span. He could barely understand what had happened to him—himself.

Matt opened his mouth to speak, but the car hop approached the window and they had to pause their conversation. His mind raced in that few moments. He wanted to help her. He really did. But here? Now? He would think of something to say, a brief version of his own experience, he supposed. He sent up a quick prayer for guidance, wisdom, for God's words to flow through him.

Chapter 15

"Glory to God in the highest heaven, and on earth peace to those on whom his favor rests." (Luke 2:14 NIV)

THANKSGIVING came and went. Jessica still had not mentioned the letter Matt had mailed to her back in early October.

Trust in the Lord with all your heart and lean not on your own understanding (Proverbs 3:5 NIV). The Scripture from Matt's early morning Bible study floated to the surface, reminding him once again to trust all things to God's timing. Christmas was right around the corner. Maybe the hope associated with the reminder of Christ's birth would trigger hope and trust in the heart of Jessica Lynn Roberts. Hope without fear.

I do trust You, Lord. Help me to not rush what could potentially be a life-long relationship with Jessica. I care too much for her to risk losing her, simply because I'm selfish and self-centered.

"Okay," he said aloud. "I'll try a less direct approach. Maybe she doesn't know me well enough yet to trust me with her whole heart. So, this weekend I will try only to win a big chunk of it. Help me to not be stupid."

Matt's vacation began on December 12, and he would not pilot another flight until January second. He was going "home." His mother had been so excited he thought she might climb right through the phone and stretch her arms around him.

"We're so grateful, Matt. How did you manage it?"

"I'm not real clear on that. But I must have some influential friends in high places that I don't know about. I put in for the time, regardless of the high traffic season, and my request was approved."

"Well, we'll take it, however we can get it. Just glad you'll be home for a while."

"Thanks, Mom. I'll see you around 6:30 Thursday evening. No need to meet the plane. I'm hoping I can talk Jess into picking me up. She isn't gone on some exotic mission I don't know about, is she?"

Catherine laughed, and the sound made Matt smile even broader. Yes, he looked forward to spending some time with his mother. His family. They had grown closer since his discharge from the Navy.

"I don't think so," said Catherine. "I invited Jessica and Marilyn to join us for Christmas Eve. Hope that's acceptable."

"You know it is."

Good. Jessica would be at the house on Christmas Eve. Matt determined right then to put a great deal of thought into the gift he would place under the tree, with Jessica's name on it.

Jessica scrolled through her e-mails, searching for a new assignment, hoping against hope that she would be able to keep her promise to spend Christmas Eve with her mom at Tommy and Catherine Churchwell's home. Out of twenty-five new messages, only one indicated a new assignment, with a target start date of January third.

"Thank You, Lord," she whispered.

She closed her laptop, glanced at her watch, then headed for the door, where she slipped on a heavy coat and lamb-lined leather gloves. If she hurried, she could just make it to H.G. before closing time.

Jessica parked in front of the store with a mere twenty minutes to spare. She loved this store. Had for years, ever since she'd come here with Kim, shopping for her stepfather. The owners took great care with every piece of clothing they custom-made. You could count on them to have everything you might possibly need for the men in your life. Plus, they paid special attention to every detail, to make your shopping experience memorable. For instance, the parking spaces and sidewalk in front of their store had been cleared and de-iced, for their customers' safety and assurance. And Jessica loved the warm lighting in the multi-framed large windows, and the bold red door that made her feel welcome, before she even got out of the car.

Jessica inhaled deeply, smiled, then made her way to the front door. Yes, this could work, even if Matt's main gift wasn't ready yet. H.G. Thrash carried everything she could hope for to accessorize. She pushed the door open and stepped inside, feeling relaxed and confident, within seconds. Everything would work out perfectly.

"Good evening. Welcome. How may we be of service?"

"I'm so sorry I'm late. Do you mind if I look around for a few minutes? I'll try not to keep you long."

"Take your time. No one is rushing you. I'll be right here, if I can help or answer any questions."

Good. With the pressure off, Jessica began to peruse the available stock. Even this close to Christmas the shelves appeared to be full. Jessica looked through the merchandise for only a few minutes, before the perfect accessory caught her eye.

"This is it," she said. "I'm ready now."

"Yes, ma'am. I'll be right there."

The sales clerk smiled as she approached Jessica.

"Thank you for your patience," said Jessica. "I'm interested in this set of cufflinks." She pointed to a stunning sterling silver pair with sapphire insets.

"Maybe you'll remember me," Jessica continued. "My name is Jessica Roberts. I placed a custom order around the first of October, and I was hoping it might be ready."

The sales clerk set the container with the cufflinks on the countertop and excused herself. She disappeared into the back room then returned shortly thereafter.

"Good news," she said. "The finishing touches were made right after lunch. Would you like to see the results?"

"Very much. Thank you."

Thank You, Lord. Matt's Christmas surprise is ready after all. When I didn't hear from the store this afternoon, I raced over here in a panic to pick out an alternate gift. I'm always jumping off some cliff or another just before the safety net is in place. Sorry. I should have waited one more day.

When the sales clerk came out carrying the dark navy, pin-striped suit in one hand, and the cream-colored Italian silk dress shirt in the other, Jessica gasped.

"It's magnificent," she said, barely above a whisper.

"We're pleased you like it," said the clerk, grinning from ear to ear. "I believe your choice of cufflinks is perfect. May I suggest a tie and pin to match?"

"Definitely," said Jessica. "Definitely."

A vision of Matthew Baldwin decked out in the most beautiful tailored suit she had ever seen took her breath away. She realized he would need to try it on and that some minor adjustments might be necessary; but that was okay. The gift would be considered extravagant to almost anyone else. But something magical was happening between her and Matt, and she wanted him to know that she knew it. She had actually enjoyed the secret she shared with Catherine alone, who had helped her obtain Matt's precise measurements, on a ruse that his mother couldn't believe how much he had filled out while in the Navy, and would he please indulge her, by allowing her to take his measurements. Jessica could still hear Catherine's giggle. Catherine had said Matt agreed, although frowning with curiosity, but had not balked at the idea. Jessica believed that tomorrow night, Matt would not be sorry that he had succumbed to his mother's request.

A fresh blanket of snow covered all of Lubbock County. Tiny lights twinkled in the branches and embraced tree trunks throughout the neighborhoods of Ransom Canyon.

Kim parked in front of her mother's home, where she stayed a good while, absorbing the heat, wondering exactly where she fit within her own family. For years, everyone had considered Matt the black sheep of the family; but Kim knew better. Granted, she didn't know everything Matt had been involved in since he'd left home; but she did know the myriad of mistakes she had made. No one knew the true depth of her rebellion.

Tears sprang to her eyes as she watched the shadows move beyond the lace sheers that hung in front of the formal dining area. She could picture the smiles on their faces; almost hear the soft voices of her mother and grandmother. Would they even notice if she didn't come inside? Would they prefer that she didn't?

Kim had set out to be the top prosecuting attorney in Lubbock and surrounding counties. Part of her believed that could still happen. In the court room, she could hold her own. But her personal life was a mess. She found herself continually slipping back into her old pattern of self-doubt. Questioning God's motives when it seemed that He'd made sure she would have to grow up without a father. Trying to find her self-worth in her career of choice, in her win-loss ratio, in the many faces of men who had snaked their way into her life. Men who all seemed to be part of a club organized to defeat her, win her heart then crush her. Leave her before a root could even sprout. Relationship challenges had begun to affect the way she responded to the slightest, harmless remark made by a family member. And she was tired of the pretense, tired of the struggle.

Kim leaned back against the seat and closed her eyes. She could imagine the room where her family had gathered for the annual Christmas Eve tradition. The ceiling of the great room stretched upward for two stories, and a ginormous Christmas tree, decked out in white and gold stood 14 feet high in the center of the room. White and gold foil-wrapped packages would take up a three-foot circle around the bottom of the tree. Her mother would never insist that everyone bring their gifts wrapped in gold and white, but most of the family had fallen into the practiced tradition. Greenery would encase the entire length of railing that protected shelf after shelf of books and movies wrapped around the open landing on the second floor. The antique barber chair that still stood in the middle of the landing would have a big red bow attached to each arm.

Catherine always went crazy with lights, inside and out. They were meant to represent the star that had appeared in the sky the night Jesus was born. Catherine had always insisted that all of the light from all of the strands, combined, would not hold a candle to that one magnificent star. Jessica had heard the story so many times she doubted she could count them all, for the birth of Jesus Christ, the story of His redemptive love, had not been reserved for Christmas alone. Not in the Baldwin household. Many a bedtime prayer had been whispered in awe at the close of the story. Kim's favorite part had been the angels bringing the good news first to the shepherds.

As Kim thought of it now, she gazed out through the windshield and whispered the prayer again. "Dear God, watch over me tonight as I close my eyes to rest. Thank You for loving me the best." Catherine had asked Kim to explain what she was thinking about when she first prayed the simple prayer, at the tender age of three. "Even when people don't like me, God always will," she'd said.

The prayer reminded Kim again, God would always love her, even when no one else did. The way she felt right now.

"Thanks, Lord, for bringing Your love into this car, where I can feel You all around me. I know, Lord, with You by my side, I can face anything. Help me realize how much You love me every day, not just tonight, not just because we have chosen this day to celebrate Your birth, no matter what calendar month in which it actually took place. December is when the entire world gets reminded of the miraculous virgin birth. The message permeates every mall, shopping center, and store, simply with the words of many traditional Christmas carols, whether shoppers realize it or not. Help me be a testimony on Your behalf, Lord. Help me get my head on straight, make better choices, and be free of the demons that plague me.

"In the name of Jesus, I rebuke Satan and his many minions, and demand they leave, for I know that they cannot dwell in the Light. Fill me with Your Spirit, Lord, and give me strength to face the next challenge."

Feeling stronger than she had in years, Kimberly Baldwin shut off the engine, opened the door, and walked toward the mansion she had called home between college graduation and the day she signed the mortgage papers on her own house. No matter where she lived now, though, 106 Arrowhead Drive would always be home. Her family had begun in this house. She had been brought home from the hospital to the upstairs nursery then slept through the escape they all made in the middle of the night, a mere two weeks later.

Piles of boxes, bows and wrapping paper littered the great room. Only two packages remained, one large box under the tree with Matt's name on it, and one small box nestled among the branches of the tree, that told the family, Jessica had one more gift to open.

All eyes were on Matt and Jessica, while they only had eyes for each other.

"Ladies first," said Matt.

"Very gracious of you, sir," said Jessica. "But, no thank you. I'm afraid you'll outshine me if I go first, and then no one will even notice what a fine job I did shopping for you."

"Is that so?"

Jessica held his gaze but did not speak again, waiting.

"Okay, I give," said Matt. "Have it your way. I'll go first."

A round of applause accompanied Jessica's move to the tree as she carefully carried the large box and placed it at Matthew's feet. They watched with great interest as Matt removed the wrapping, showing little regard for the ribbon or the bright red paper. It seemed an amazing coincidence that Matt and Jessica had both strayed from the white and gold tradition, and wrapped one gift to each other, in red.

Matt placed the long flat box across his lap, dug out his pocket knife and slit the tape that secured the sides, then gasped as he spread apart the tissue paper that concealed the garments below.

Catherine squealed from the other side of the room. She made her way over to the tree, at a quick pace.

"Oh, Jessica," she cried. "It's magnificent!"

"It is, isn't it?"

"Do us a favor, Matthew," said Catherine. "Try it on."

Matt didn't answer his mother. He stared at Jessica.

"Jess."

"You're welcome. Every man needs a nice suit. If you'll look underneath, there are a few accessories to complete the ensemble."

"Nice doesn't begin to describe it."

"I did good, huh?"

Jessica stood beside Matthew, grinning down at him.

Matt set the box aside, stood, and turned toward her. "You're really something, you know that?"

"It's the only thing I could think of."

"It's perfect."

"I'm glad you like it. Thank Catherine too, though. She finagled the measurements for me."

Matt finally turned and acknowledged his mother's presence.

"I knew you were being sneaky," he said. "But this is over the top. Thank you."

"I agree that it's perfect. And you're welcome."

They shared a hug then Matt faced Kimberly once again.

"You ready to outshine me?"

"I'm ready."

"I can hardly wait," said Catherine.

"Here here," said James. "Get on with it."

Matt smiled, his eyes on Jessica. He planted a kiss on her cheek as he reached up into the center of the tree. He took the small shiny package down and handed it to Jessica.

"Matt."

"I think you'll like it," he said.

Jessica unwrapped the gift by feel, never taking her eyes off Matt's face. She blinked, hard, and took in a deep breath when her fingers touched the velvet box.

"It's okay, Jess," said Matt, as he bent to whisper in her ear. "Don't be afraid."

Jessica looked up to see love looking back at her. Not the desperate kind of love that would frighten anyone. But a look of love that seemed to reach deep into her soul. No, she would not be afraid to open the little velvet box. No matter what. She felt ready for what the Lord had for them to share in the future.

And so, she opened the box with faith and great anticipation.

When Jessica peeked inside the box, she could only smile, even broader than she'd been smiling all evening. She didn't know whether to laugh with relief or cry in disappointment. Of course, she suspected an engagement ring, but at the same time, she did not wish to be proposed to in front of the entire family. But the pair of half-karat diamond earrings that glistened from its velveteen setting, although not what she had anticipated, made her heart swell and her eyes leak.

A tear escaped and crawled down her face.

"It's perfect, Matt. Perfect."

"Well, it's a step, anyway."

Chapter 16

For I am about to fall, and my pain is ever with me. I confess my iniquity; I am troubled by my sin (Psalm 88:17 NIV).

KIM slammed the door behind her. With trembling hands, she fumbled with the dead bolts, desperate to secure all of them.

At last, she heard the last lock click into place then slid to the floor, her back supported by the wooden hunter green barrier that protected her from the man on the other side. The night pressed in on her. The memory still fresh. She could hear him laughing at her. Jeering at her. Pushing her down hard against the carpet on his office floor.

Just like many other late nights, Kim let the tears fall. But no night had been exactly like this one.

It had started innocently enough. A well-respected attorney from a prominent family had noticed her. They had spoken a few times in the lobby of the courthouse. And the admiration in his eyes served well to feed her ego.

Then, months later, he'd kissed her casually at a New Year's Eve party on the balcony of his parents' home. The night had been frigid, and he'd offered her his overcoat, which swallowed her small frame. They had lunch January third, went to dinner January seventh, and on January twenty-first, he escorted her to the Lubbock Symphony Orchestra.

Kimberly had begun to feel confident that the future would be brighter than the past. Since coming clean with her emotions before the Lord on Christmas Eve, she had spent every spare moment reading her Bible and conversing with God. It felt really good to give her life over to His control. She very much wanted things to be different. For other people to see how she'd changed. For men to no longer seek her company because she had a reputation for falling for every tired old line used to trap a lady, and compromise her integrity. She had vowed to quit taking dating so lightly, and to demand respect from anyone who wanted to share her company.

And Dirk Johnson III seemed to fit the bill perfectly. He had been nothing but polite—opened doors for her, held her coat, and treated her with the kind of admiration and gentility she had only dreamed of. And he was older, obviously more mature than the other arrogant attorneys she had kept company with.

A blizzard-plagued night at the symphony had become a pleasant, memorable evening—right up until ten minutes after they arrived to see the interior decorating that had recently transformed his office.

Their date turned ugly in a hurry. Afterward, Kim cried all the way home, while the well-bred attorney mocked her without mercy. He slowed to a near-stop in front of her house, and waited only until Kim's foot touched the curb before he sped away, letting the car door slam on its own.

Much as she resisted it, Kim heard the always-proper voice of her big sister, Brooke, echoing through the years. It crashed into her head with the force of yesterday's ever-present memory, as though Brooke had entered Kim's house and stood over her with a stern look.

"I know you like him, Kimmie," Brooke would say. "And I agree that he's cute. But this one is not trustworthy. I happen to know. For a fact."

Brooke's voice in Kim's head prompted that long-ago answer she still found herself trying to prove:

"I believe I am capable of judging a person's character for myself, Brooke," she'd said. "You have been calling interference for me quite long enough."

"Suit yourself." Kim could almost hear Brooke's voice. "But if you continue on this course you will learn the hard way that I know what I'm talking about."

Ever since, Kim had been learning the hard way—over and over again.

For the next few minutes, Kim sat in the floor and cried. It wasn't supposed to be this way. She had tried super hard to be selective and discerning; but Dirk had fooled her beyond anything she could have imagined.

"How could I be so stupid? Every time I fall for a guy, I believe the same cruel lies. I thought You heard me, Lord. Why is this happening to me?"

Another Saturday night date in shreds. Only no date had ended with Kim being violated, forced to do the unmentionable, used and abused at the same time. Not since the divorce, had anyone violated her or beaten her. Yes, she had been slapped a few times, and forced to kiss someone whose manners repulsed her, but those experiences paled in comparison. Not even the abuse of her ex-husband could compare with the humiliation that shattered her very soul tonight.

She felt helpless, alone, and afraid. She cried out to the Lord again. "Why, Lord?"

Do not be afraid, My child. I am with you.

The voice Kim heard in her heart seemed real, genuine, and encouraging. But she needed help; and she needed it now.

She didn't dare call her mother. If she did, most of the family would materialize on her doorstep in less than an hour. And it wouldn't do any good to call Matt. He lived too far away.

But she suddenly remembered one person she had always been able to count on. Someone who would keep her secret, and help her through this. She could call Jess.

Kim didn't try to get up, just reached inside her purse for the cell phone. Jessica picked up on the third ring.

"Kim, it's so late. Are you okay?"

Kim began to cry.

"Don't say another word. I'm on my way."

Jessica knew Kim had been disappointed by boyfriends she'd had since the divorce; but she had not cried out to her best friend before. Not once.

Jessica didn't know if Kim had called anyone else; but the family knew something unsettled still lingered within the heart of Kimberly Margaret Baldwin. Maggie had tried to talk to Kim in the not too distant past; but Kim had laughed it off with a casual shrug.

"Some people find their true love easier than others, Maggie. Nothing to concern yourself about."

Maggie had said she didn't believe that for a second, but Kim refused to budge, and the subject had been dropped.

Jessica knew better, as well. She and Kim had had a few lunches together, when Kim refused to discuss her love life. Would avoid any offer Jessica might make when it came to blind dates, or double dates, or any mention of men, in general. Something peculiar, or awful, must have been going on with Kim that she chose not to share. Something sinister that caused Kim to shrink inside herself, change the subject, or excuse herself and leave, lunch notwithstanding.

Jessica had wondered if Kim's poor choices in men stemmed from the pain of growing up without a father, or from the nightmare of being kidnapped while they were college students. Or if she had been so emotionally bruised by her first husband that she could no longer see her own self-worth.

It was difficult to say what went on in the heart and mind of another human being. But Kim's behavior bordered on the ridiculous, like she was trying to punish herself for some conceived sin she had never committed. Some flaw God had known about in advance, and thus punished her before she was ever born. After all, He'd let her father die, before she had even met him. Kim had confessed as much.

The whole thing didn't make any sense. Jessica believed it might take some serious Christian counseling to clear up the past enough that Kim could look it in the face, deal with it, and then leave it back there—where it belonged.

Kim had a good reputation as an attorney, well-respected and appreciated by her clients. She had connections with judges and law enforcement officers—and a tendency to blame herself for being unlovable, unworthy, and too trusting. No one had been able to crack the shell she had cloaked herself with.

The phone call scared Jessica. Something must be terribly wrong, for Kim to reach out.

Jessica pulled into Kim's driveway with great care. The alley stayed shady during the day and remained much more hazardous than the front. The January wind whipped snow across the hood of Jessica's car as she rolled up to the garage door. She used the just-in-case garage door opener she had managed to get from Kim the year before, when she'd asked Kim to keep a spare key to her own apartment. Just in case. Trying to talk Kim into doing what you thought best for her, almost never worked. But if you could make her believe your good idea had originated with her, you were golden.

The garage door lifted and Jessica parked under its protection, grateful she did not have to stand out in the cold. When Kim bought the property, Jessica thought she was being extravagant and frivolous.

"I will be entertaining, Jess," she'd said. "You can't invite a group of attorneys to a gathering in just any old place."

"I'm sure that's true, Madam Kimberly."

Jessica had teased her at the time, but the extravagance had served Kimberly well. Evidently, she'd been right. From the outside, it seemed that a budding attorney could make or break her social standing with one poorly-administered festivity. Social standing came long before the money started rolling in on a regular basis. Evidently.

Jessica hurried to Kim's back door. She knocked once, and the door flew open. Jessica stared at her friend.

"What in the world?"

Kimberly broke down. She hadn't looked in a mirror, or left her spot by the front door, until she heard the garage door open. She managed to push herself up, stand, then force one foot in front of the other down the entryway, across the living and dining areas. She reached the back door just as Jessica knocked on the other side.

Kim backed away from her friend, inching toward the dinette then collapsed onto the cushioned seat of one of the four dining chairs. Jessica followed and took the seat opposite Kim.

Kim lowered her head in her hands and wept. Her shoulders shook with her sobbing. After a long five minutes, Kim dropped her hands and raised her tear-streaked face to Jessica.

"He hurt me, Jess, in a way I've never been hurt before. He said I asked for it, because I wore a strapless dress under a short jacket, and my hem hit above my knees."

"He?"

"Yes."

"Who?"

Tears filled her eyes again, but Kim just shook her head. "I can't tell you," she said.

"Okay. So tell the police. Tell Matt."

"Tell Matt! Are you crazy? Matt would kill him."

"Maybe. And maybe he would just make sure this criminal turned himself in."

"I'm not telling Matt. And I'm not calling the police. He's from a prominent family. He'd just deny it; and I'd be ruined. I think I may have to leave Lubbock County altogether."

Jessica could hardly believe what she was hearing. A man had forced himself on her friend, and Kim had decided not to press charges because he was from a prominent family? No way. She had to think fast. There had to be a way to convince Kim she *wanted* to make the call.

"Mind if I ask a question or two, if I promise not to ask his name?"

"I don't promise to answer," said Kim.

"Just general questions."

"Okay."

"How old is he?"

"Forty-something. I'm not sure."

"Married?"

"No."

"Ever been married?"

"I don't think so."

"And his family is from Lubbock?"

"Ever since there has been a Lubbock."

"Is he an attorney?"

Kim clamped her lips shut tight.

"Okay, that does it," said Jessica. "I know who did this to you."

"You do not."

"Yes, I do. I've been a nosey reporter long enough to know a little about what gets swept under the rug in this county. And I know you're not his first victim."

Jessica had been at the crime scene more than a few times. A beautiful young attorney, fallen under his spell, then fallen victim to his brutal attack. No official charges had ever been filed. And it had happened more than a few times.

Jessica reached across the table and touched Kim's hand. She jumped.

"Kimberly," whispered Jessica. "How many more girls will you allow this creep to hurt?"

Kimberly Margaret Baldwin had grown up without a dad and with two moderately protective brothers, one fiercely protective brother, and a sister who tried to shelter her from her own definition of unsavory characters.

As an adult, Kim had fallen into a pattern of not telling her family much of anything about her social life. No buffer existed to tell her what to expect. No alarm sounded with approaching danger. If a man flirted with her, admired her professionally, or invited her to lunch, she responded with enthusiasm. Every time. The need to be loved, almost overwhelming.

One after another she accepted dates with overly aggressive, or insanely possessive, men. If you asked her, she would probably deny it, for she had no idea why she kept sabotaging herself. Dominant men who ultimately showed their disdain for a feminine version of themselves, who could hold her own in a court of law. It seemed as though they felt compelled to beat her at something. Force her into their concept of feminism. Or something just as ludicrous.

Kimberly Baldwin had quickly built a reputation as a criminal prosecutor. She had been trusted with cases for the underdog, as a junior associate. She boldly stood up for the rights of victims, and didn't stop digging until she found the truth. And didn't stop arguing until the scumbags went to jail.

But in her personal life, Kim remained the victim. Each man more forceful and domineering than the last.

And now she sat across from her best friend, defeated and crushed, afraid to stand up for herself.

"I don't think I can do it," said Kim.

"And I don't think your conscience will let you do anything less."

Jessica pulled out her cell phone, slid it across the table then stopped it directly in front of Kim.

Chapter 17

Trust in the LORD with all your heart and lean not on your own understanding; in all your ways submit to him, and he will make your paths straight (Proverbs 3:5-6 NIV).

JESSICA woke to the smell of what she recognized to be turkey bacon and coffee. She smiled, remembering. Thanks to Eunice Mae Howell, Jessica not only loved the smell of coffee, but now looked forward to a cup every morning, complete with Half & Half and organic stevia, just like Eunice Mae had taught her.

"Good morning, sleepy head," said Kim. "How would you like your eggs?"

"Is it late?"

"Nine o'clock."

"Guess I was tired."

"Guess so. Scrambled?"

"If they're not juicy."

"Got it."

Jessica made her way to the Keurig. She then moved to the small dinette set with her doctored coffee and let Kim do her thing at the grill. Kimberly was one of those rare combinations—attorney and chef. Kim had agreed to cook Jessica's meat well done and her eggs hard, because otherwise, Jessica wouldn't eat. But the plate, the stoneware or china, decidedly came decorated with a sprig of parsley, fresh slices of tomato, and juice served in fine crystal.

That was Kim.

And Jessica loved her. And she would do whatever it took to put Dirk Johnson III behind bars. Kimberly might have some issues to work through, but she didn't deserve what that troglodyte had done to her. No one deserved that.

Kim sat across from Jessica, sipped her coffee, and nibbled at her food.

"What is it, Kim? Something bothering you?"

"No. But I do need to say something."

Jessica put her fork down.

"I'm listening."

"Good. Because I'm going with you."

"Kim."

"Don't 'Kim' me. I'm not going to sit around this house twiddling my thumbs, while you're risking your life for me."

Jessica put a forkful of egg in her mouth to keep from responding right away. She really didn't want to have to worry about keeping up with Kimberly in the field. But she couldn't blame her for wanting to be in the thick of things either. If their positions were reversed they would have to tie Jessica to a chair to keep her cooped up in this house. Jessica chewed slowly, thoughtfully. Finally resigned to the idea, she swallowed and laid the fork on the edge of the plate then looked Kimberly in the eye.

"Tommy will probably turn both of us over his knee."

"Thank you, Jess. I won't be in the way, I promise. I have some research skills of my own, you know. I spent three years of law school in and out of a research library. And since then, I've learned a lot about digging up answers the other side didn't think I could find, much less use against them."

"Perfect."

"You won't be sorry," said Kim.

"I just hope we aren't both sorry."

Kim could tell through the heavy glass panes that Matt stood on the other side of the door. If he could have taken off work two days earlier, he would have been there two days earlier. He rang the bell a second time. Kim knew it, and appreciated it, but dreaded the confrontation, nonetheless. She had begged Jessica not to call him. Jessica called him anyway.

"Keep your shirt on," she muttered. "I'm coming."

When Kim opened the door, Matt surprised her. Tears pooled in his eyes, and he didn't speak for several seconds. Not an immediate dive into a scorching lecture, but real concern for his baby sister, showed on his face.

"Mind if I come in?" he said at last.

Kim stood back and held the door open wide for her brother. He stepped inside and looked down at her.

"How can I help?"

"Come in. We'll talk."

Matt didn't move from the spot just inside the foyer, but opened his arms to his sister. Kim fell into them like the sanctuary she knew they would be. His arms, gentle and loving, enfolded her. She remembered how much she loved him, and missed their long talks and silly antics. In that moment, Kim missed being just his baby sister. She relaxed against his broad chest and let him hold her while she cried.

The firm had granted Kim a six-month leave of absence; but she expected the nightmare to go on much longer than that...

She had taken Jessica's advice and called the police within an hour of Dirk the Jerk's (her new nickname for him) attack, so the examination proved helpful. The humiliation of being questioned and examined would definitely leave a mental scar. The fact that Dirk's father happened to be a retired District Judge only aggravated the situation.

Dirk Johnson III had charmed and chafed more young girls than his father would likely be willing to admit. But apparently, he'd sheltered Dirk long enough. Dad had called the police station and declared his son would no longer be coddled. He would own up to his crimes and go to prison, if it came to that. Judge Johnson's declaration had caused no small stir.

Even so, Jessica feared for Kim's life. Anything could happen. Judge Johnson could change his mind or simply be persuaded by some illogical crisis of conscience to use his remaining power and influence to get Dirk off the hook. Again. If that happened, and Dirk were set free, Jessica believed he would come after Kim. And kill her.

Kim led Matt into the living room and let out a low whistle.

"Nice digs, sis. You win the Lottery?"

"Ha ha. You know I don't buy Lotto tickets. It is a nice place though, isn't it?"

Matt had noticed a small den/office to his right when he came in the front door. Fine pieces of art work graced the entry walls and the living room. Oversized furniture he recognized as the Binette Italia line, his mother's favorite, filled the living and dining areas. The entrance to the master bedroom opened at the back of the living room. A glance inside the master bedroom showed more of the same. Heavy wrought iron patio furniture could be seen through the patio doors to his right.

"A little pricy, don't you think, Kimmie?"

"No student loans."

"Yeah, right. All I know is, you better be one heck of a lawyer so you can pay off your mortgage and your furniture debt."

Kim stood with her hands on her hips and glared at him.

"I *am* one heck of an attorney," she said, "and I have no debt."

Matt held up both arms in surrender. Evidently, Matt didn't know about the trust fund that had been set up by their grandmother after her kidnapping. It did not come into play until she graduated law school, and she had been relatively frugal with its contents. Whether Kimberly Margaret Baldwin ever worked another case in her life, she would not be hurting for money.

"I don't doubt it," he said. "On either count. Now, let's get down to what happens next. You're not going to stay here alone, are you?"

"No, she's not," said Jessica, entering the room from the same way Matt had come earlier.

"Jess. Where did you come from?"

"Not that it's any of your business," she said, "but I just left the rest room that is in the hall outside the guest bedroom."

"Oh. Sorry."

"No problem. The bedroom and bath are just to the left of the front door. You probably didn't notice. Anyway, I've been staying with Kim since the night she was attacked. And I'll be here till they lock up Dirk Johnson III. And I plan to do my dead-level best to convince some more of his victims to file charges, as well."

Matt still could not believe this was happening. Guilt pressed in on him, because he had not had that heart-to-heart talk with Maggie.

He had not bothered to make his sister take the time to talk to him. He had left her on her own, for years, knowing full well how much she had relied upon him to be there for her. And now, this Dirk fellow had hurt her. How many more times had she been hurt? How bad had it been for her when she got divorced while he was overseas? Little Kimmie. A child without a father. And for years, a child without the support of her closest sibling.

Kim, Matt and Jessica came together at the dining room table to discuss the particulars of her ongoing safety—before, during and after the trial.

"Who will be here with Kim when you are out on assignment, Jess?"

"I have taken a leave of absence. But even as we speak, Mother, Tommy and Ms. Eunice are pooling their resources to provide around-the-clock security, so it doesn't matter whether I am here or not, Kim will be safe."

"Around the clock? I didn't see anyone out there when I pulled up."

"Excellent. You would have known it, if you hadn't matched any of the pictures we gave the security company. There are only a handful of people who can safely approach Kim's door."

Matt raised his brows.

"Good to know I'm on the list. I'll sleep better knowing there is security in place. Just wish I didn't live so far away. But don't hesitate to call if you need me to come running. I'll figure out a way to get here."

"Thanks, Matt," said Kim. "I really missed you all those years you were gone."

"I missed you, too. I don't know everything that happened to you while I was overseas, Kimmie, but I think it's time we leave it all back there. The future does not have to be a reflection of the past. Understand?"

"I understand. I was working on that very thing, when this happened. It may take some doing, but I intend to get some Christian counseling to help change the nightmare my life has morphed into."

Matt closed his eyes and whispered a prayer of thanksgiving.

"And we'll all be here to help," said Jessica.

"Yes, we will," said Matt, as he reached a hand out toward Jessica and one toward Kim. "Let's pray right now. I feel like we need to start this investigation off on the right foot."

Matt looked deep into the eyes of Jessica Roberts. He hated the miles that separated them, especially now. Walking away would not be easy. They stood under Kimberly's porch light. He loved being with his two favorite girls—his baby sister, and the girl he had fallen for in a big way. Jessica held his heart, and it felt...right. The women who had tried to own him had driven him away. But this girl, independent, feisty, and bold, had allowed him to chase her, allowed him the space most men appreciate. But the more space she offered him, the less he wanted to be away from her.

"I don't have to tell you to be careful, do I?"

"Well, not again, anyway." Jessica laughed. She seemed completely at ease with herself.

Mostly, Matt loved that about her. But Dirk Johnson had spent decades bullying women, breaking the law, and getting away with it. Just because he was behind bars at the moment wasn't much comfort. He could have some pretty rough characters who followed his directions, simply because it paid well.

"Matt, this is what I do. Remember?"

"I remember; but I don't trust Dirk Johnson."

He smiled down at her and brushed her cheek with the back of his hand. "If anything happened to you, I'd."

"Shhhh," said Jessica, placing her finger on his lips. "I'm not going at this without backup, you know."

"Yes, I know. But."

The thought of a world without the light of Jessica Roberts in it threatened to crush his spirit. Matt had fallen hard for this young, beautiful, crazy reporter. He longed to take her in this arms and show her just how much she meant to him—so much more than the diamond earrings he'd given her for Christmas could convey. But today would not be that day. At this point, all his power lay in the power of prayer. Mere common sense would not be nearly enough to sway her.

"No buts. I promise to follow protocol, and keep the authorities posted, to text you with updates, and to pretend I don't know Tommy hired someone to follow me everywhere I go."

She smiled up at him.

"I didn't know you knew that part."

And he didn't care. He and Tommy had agreed on this strategy shortly after Jessica announced her intention to bring down Dirk Johnson—single-handedly, if necessary. They both knew she was bullheaded enough to jump into the ring with him, and whatever minions climbed in there with them. Matt loved her spirit; but it might also be the scariest thing about her.

"Okay. I give," he said, raising both hands in surrender. "I'm going back to work now. However, you can expect me to put in for vacation time, if this doesn't get wrapped up in a few weeks, without incident."

"Okay. But give me at least six, would you?"

"I'll try."

He grinned in spite of the worrisome nag in his chest. Sometimes Jessica could be a little too brave for his comfort.

Jessica stood under the porch light and watched Matthew pull away from the curb, roll down to the end of the cul-de-sac, make a U-turn, idle for a moment in front of her, then wave as he reached the corner to turn right. Tonight, looking into his eyes, she was totally okay with having a future with Matthew Baldwin. She reached up and fiddled with one of the earrings Matt had given her for

Christmas, remembering the kiss they had shared in front of the entire family. She smiled again, content. In her heart, she knew the next diamond would fit her left ring finger. Jessica was growing more and more fond of the idea; but God would have to be in charge of the timing. Although she could dream tonight, tomorrow she would hit the streets running. She had a criminal to bring down. A monster who had lived outside the law far too long. A creep—who gave her the creeps.

Jessica went back inside, closed the door, and diligently secured the deadbolts, before making her way to the front bedroom. Kim had long since turned in. They had hashed and rehashed every angle they could think of to hurry along the investigation, to give Kimberly's attorney all the ammunition they could muster, before Dirk's case went to trial.

Jessica doubled-down on her reporting skills. She called in favors and hounded the editor-in-chief of the *Avalanche Journal* until he agreed to assign a research project to one of his rookie reporters. And she started asking lots of questions in lots of places, beginning with the Texas Tech School of Law. She tracked down every female graduate since Dirk Johnson III had been a student there. She took half the leads and trusted the *Journal* reporter with the other half.

Chapter 18

The Lord is with me; I will not be afraid. What can mere mortals do to me?
(Psalm 118:6 NIV).

TWO WEEKS later, Matt called to see what Kim and Jessica's search had turned up. Jessica had already had this conversation with Tommy and Catherine; but she was willing to explain it all again. How, out of a myriad of law students who had attended Texas Tech University School of Law around the same time as Dirk Johnson III, and many, many more since he'd graduated, only five remained in Lubbock County. And how disappointing their findings.

"Out of the five, three agreed to meet with me," said Jessica. "They don't know why yet. I didn't dare play that card, or we'd be back at square one already."

The *Avalanche Journal* connection had proven invaluable. Ex-students would talk to a local reporter they thought could further their career as an attorney. Once the reporter met these ladies face-to-face, he would drop the Dirk Johnson ball. With any luck the plan wouldn't backfire on them. They needed some witnesses to corroborate Kim's portrayal of Dirk's character. The more proof they had, the more time Dirk would spend behind bars.

"How soon is the first interview?" said Matt.

"Next Tuesday. Then one on Thursday, and one on Friday. I hope we get what we're looking for. Next week will be the end of my leave. I have a new assignment waiting for me the following Monday."

Jessica felt almost desperate to help Kimberly before she had to fly overseas again. Even one girl willing to testify that Dirk had forced her into a compromising position, had abused her then sent her away, disgraced and undone, would make a world of difference. Just one.

Matt interrupted her musings.

"I'll be praying for all of you. If I can help let me know."

"Thank you. We're for sure going to need the prayers; and I'll definitely call, especially if things go haywire."

One interview followed another. One question after another, yet no progress had been made by the following Friday afternoon. Even though each girl had been aware that Dirk sat securely behind bars, they refused to utter a word against him in a court of law.

"I'm sorry, Kimberly. Really. I couldn't get even one of them to agree to testify."

It broke Jessica's heart to say it. But she had to get back to work. She had managed to get a continued commitment out of the rookie reporter, Kevin Hooper, to keep digging, to keep trying to convince one of Dirk's victims to do the right thing—but that's all they could do, for now. Somewhere, a woman existed who would be willing to help bring Dirk the Jerk down.

Kim fiddled with the edge of her napkin, trying to control her emotions. She wanted to hunt the other girls down and scream them into submission. Part of her wanted to go so far as to threaten them. How could so many women refuse to come forward when they *must* know that Dirk Johnson had abused untold numbers of girls, had obviously forced them into submission?

But it didn't matter, did it? Kim could put him away all by herself. The physician's report, the police report, all the evidence that had been gathered, would end his crime spree. Right?

Maybe. But not for nearly so long a sentence as he deserved. Not near.

Kim looked up into Jessica's eyes.

"It's not your fault. It's mine. I've made careless choices, over and over again. It was bound to catch up with me."

Jessica frowned, and Kim cringed. She deserved whatever her friend said next. Jessica's next move, however, surprised Kimberly, bringing a rush of tears to the surface.

Jessica reached across the table and gripped Kim's hand, holding her with her eyes.

"Going out with a guy—any guy—does not warrant the kind of mistreatment that has been forced on you."

Tears spilled over onto Kim's cheeks, and she let them fall. She couldn't count the number of times she had blamed herself for the poor way she had been treated by men she thought she could trust. Trust, the way her mother had trusted her daddy; and now, the way her mother trusted Tommy. The way her grandparents had trusted each other.

Kim still had to fight the anger that swelled within her when she thought of her father. She had been two weeks old when he passed away from a brain aneurysm, lost to her forever. However, the father she would never know had poured out his love for her in a journal. Once she discovered it and read its contents, her curiosity had been satisfied. Yes, her father had loved her. As much as anyone could love an unborn child, anyway. But all the love she would ever receive from him amounted to a few strokes of ink in a book. She would never feel her hand in his, or hear his voice, or his unique laugh that Brooke had tried so hard to describe. She would never share the memories her siblings had of a loving, godly, playful dad. So, no matter how hard she tried, she would never be like the other kids in the family.

Maybe she tried a little too hard to find love. Maybe she looked in all the wrong places. But one day, she determined with all her being, she would find forever love. God would help her with that, wouldn't He? Especially since she had surrendered her life anew, seen the error of her ways, and had proceeded with caution before going out on a date again. With anyone. She had tried so hard. Been so sure.

"Listen to me, Kimberly," said Jessica, interrupting Kim's train of thought. "I am your friend. Always have been, always will be. No matter what. And I'll be here for you to the very end. Whatever it takes to figure out why you are drawn to these low-life scumbags, I'll help you through it. Only don't ever blame yourself. In my opinion, they should all be hanged."

Kim couldn't stop the laughter that bubbled up out of her, a laugh mingled with tears. She felt relief and guilt and fear, all jumbled up in one big wad of emotion.

"I'm serious," said Jessica. "There's no good excuse for treating a lady with disrespect, much less being overbearing and abusive."

"Tell me about it."

"Anyway, I have an assignment I can no longer ignore, so I hope you'll forgive me for skipping out on you. The kid from the *Journal* promised to keep digging, and I'll get back as soon as I can. If you need anything right away, call Tommy. If you need Matt, call him. He'll come running. Got it?"

"Yes, ma'am. Thank you, again, for coming to the rescue."

"Wouldn't have been anywhere else. Now, take care of yourself, and don't do anything stupid. Sorry, sweetie, but I gotta run."

Kim felt her heart sink. Saying goodbye to Jessica would be harder than she'd thought. They had grown close over the past weeks. Even closer than when they shared classes and adventures during their college years. They were all grown up now, and their relationship had expanded to encompass the trials of adulthood. Even though invisible eyes would still be watching Kim's house, the emptiness would feel much more empty without her friend to talk to, to bounce ideas off of. To just not be alone.

"I understand," said Kim, forcing herself to be upbeat. "Don't worry. Everything will turn out for the best. I just know it."

"That's better," said Jessica. "Keep that attitude and it really will turn out for the best. But I have to ask you to do something for me. Please don't go out alone, Kimberly. Let Kevin do his job. Take up an indoor hobby, surf the Internet, read, pray. But promise me you won't go out alone."

The look in Kimberly's eyes stabbed Jessica in the heart.

"I'll hate it," Kim said, after a long, uncomfortable pause. "But I promise. Be safe on your assignment, and don't you do anything stupid, either. I'll be praying for you."

Their goodbye was mixed with a longing that one could protect the other, that life would give them both a break. That God would send a host of angels to protect Kimberly in Lubbock County, and Jessica on the other side of the world.

The newspaper shook in her hands as Allison McNew read beyond the headlines to take in the full article. She could barely believe what she was reading. Someone had stepped up and filed charges against Dirk Johnson III. The reporter had made it clear that the prosecution needed testimonies in support of Kimberly Baldwin's claims against his character. A strong case would be needed to bring down the son of one of Lubbock County's most prestigious judges.

Allison had humbled herself to the point of humiliation. Had cried and pleaded and promised, but to no avail. Neither Dirk Johnson III, nor his father, had any sympathy for a girl with loose morals, and flatly refused to help her in any way. Not financially, emotionally, or with support further down the line. She had managed to get pregnant outside of wedlock. How could they be sure the baby had been fathered by Dirk III? If she would give herself to one man, why not several? And if she filed charges against Dirk, she would be more than sorry. They had made that very clear. Allison had no idea what that meant; but the threat had convinced her to run.

Allison McNew, an orphan with no family to run to, had been forced to drop out of the Texas Tech University School of Law and figure out how to have a baby on her own, work a job, and raise her child—alone.

"What's so interesting?" said Summer, Allison's fifteen-year-old daughter who had been born in August, almost exactly on her due date, nine months to the day from the night Dirk had date-raped young, unsuspecting Allison McNew. Drugged her with something he'd added to the first drink she'd had in her young life. A second-year law student, Allison had survived high school and college without burning her throat with so much as a beer—and with her virginity intact. Then this monster of a man had not only taken that delicate treasure from her, but had taken her future right along with it.

Allison broke away from the newspaper article and the memories, and smiled at her daughter, who looked exactly like her father.

"Good morning, sweetie. Sleep good?"

"Yes, ma'am. What are you reading? I haven't seen you this interested in anything out of Lubbock, Texas, well, in forever."

Allison closed the newspaper and made eye contact with her daughter.

"Have a seat, baby. It's time I told you the truth."

Dirk Johnson's trial would begin on Monday. Allison made some phone calls to rearrange her schedule. She spoke to Summer's teachers so they could take her assignments with them. She then gathered up all the evidence she had organized against Dirk over the years, stuffed it in an over-sized briefcase, and set out for the airport. With no weather delays, they should be able to get from Nashville, Tennessee to Lubbock, Texas, settle into a hotel, and meet with the *Avalanche Journal* reporter, by Tuesday afternoon.

Allison believed with all her heart that this time, Dirk Johnson III would be the one crying and pleading for mercy. And she would watch his fall with dry eyes, and a tight grip on her daughter's hand.

Chapter 19

Rescue me, LORD, from evildoers; protect me from the violent, who devise evil plans in their hearts and stir up war every day (Psalm 140:1-2 NIV).

JESSICA stood at the balcony of her hotel suite in downtown San Francisco, a furrow marking her once-serene brow. She had been ferociously busy the past five days, and had not stopped to think about the circumstances that had led to her acceptance of this particular assignment. She hadn't even taken the time to get an update on Kimberly's situation. Had Dirk already been tried, convicted, and put away, where he couldn't hurt anyone for a good long time? Or had he been released, yet again, and left free to roam the city and continue to devour young women, without consequence?

And how was her best friend dealing with being alone? Had she been required to face Dirk in open court? Or had his attorney managed to get him off, altogether? Frustrated, Jessica blew out a breath and vowed to call Kim before noon. She had been on back-to-back assignments since February.

But now, with the whirlwind behind her, Jessica could see through the early morning fog, across the water beyond The Rock, and into her living room in Lubbock, Texas. The memory greatly disturbed her. The frown on Matt's face hadn't set well on her stomach; and following the confrontation, it had churned halfway to California...

"You'll just have to trust me," said Jessica. "I do have a brain, you know."

"I'm not disputing *your* mental capacity," said Matt. "But do you realize what kind of maniac you will be dealing with over there?"

"I don't know yet. We haven't been formally introduced."

She knew she sounded stubborn, rude even, but at the moment, she didn't care.

"Well, I know something about him. And I can tell you, emphatically, he is not a nice man. I know for a fact that his company sold guns, *American-made* guns, to the enemy in Afghanistan. A man with so little respect for our country has no business within 500 miles of you. Trust me, he will have no respect for you either."

Looking back, she had to admit, Matt had been right. Her life had been spared, only because of a last-minute rescue manned by the FBI...

An angry man in a lab coat stood over the gurney Jessica had been strapped to. Her eyes were getting heavy as the sedative began to take effect.

How had this happened? She questioned herself, even as she felt her mind drifting into oblivion. She had arrived for the interview with Mark Huckabee precisely as scheduled. She had been escorted into a waiting room, where she sat for two hours before the man she had arranged to meet, arrived on the scene.

Jessica jumped to her feet as Mr. Huckabee entered the room.

"Mr. Huckabee," she began.

"Be seated," he said.

"But I have been waiting..."

A man came up behind her and forced her into the chair. He shoved her hard, and her temper flared. She glared at him and started to speak.

Mark held up his hand to stop her.

"I know who you are and I know you were sent here undercover at the request of Matthew Baldwin," he said. "But I don't know why you've come. What exactly did you expect to learn?"

Matthew Baldwin? What did Matt have to do with any of this?

"I have no idea what you're talking about. I simply came to learn the truth. I am on assignment with *Time* magazine. Matthew Baldwin has nothing to do with it."

The man stared at her for a long moment, his eyes narrowed, his fists clenched at his sides.

"What makes you think there is a truth to be discovered? And you are lying about Matthew Baldwin. I am aware of your relationship with him."

"Seriously? There are pages and pages of speculation all over the Internet about your corporation, your overseas deals, your honor, or lack thereof." Her voice cranked up a notch. "And Matthew Baldwin has nothing to do with my being here!"

His laugh was loud, long, and evil.

Jessica tried to stand again; but half-way up she was slammed back down, so hard it made her head swim. Seconds later, she felt a needle jammed into the side of her neck.

Jessica woke three days later in an office of the FBI, on Golden Gate Avenue, in San Francisco.

She looked around the room—a room filled with books and a large oval conference table. She really had no idea what had happened to her, or how she had ended up in this room. But at least she was alone. No angry men stared at her, or threatened her, or...

She stood on shaky legs, pushing the thought out of her head. Remembering made her head hurt. She made her way to the pitcher of water on a side table, and poured herself a glass, calmly, as though nothing out of the ordinary had happened. She moved to the wall of windows, looked out over the city, and sipped the cool water, wondering how she had ended up in this building. Wondering who had saved her. And how. And why.

Something told her she would not be alone for long. But it gave her a few minutes to wrap her head around everything she'd been through, what it might mean to her future as a photo journalist; and how Matt might react to this latest episode. If she kept putting herself in harm's way, it could cost her more than a career. It could cost her—her life. And even if she managed to survive, it could cost her Matthew Baldwin. Was any job, any story, worth such a high price?

The door opened behind her. She did not turn around.

"Jess."

Matt!

Jessica turned slowly around, her eyes wide.

"Matt."

"Are you okay?" he said, moving a step closer.

"I'm fine," said Jessica. "A little confused. Who called you?"

"The Director."

"Of the FBI?"

Matt chuckled, but nodded his head.

"Let's get back to my original question. Are you okay?"

Jessica started toward him, but paused at the head of the conference table. She looked Matt straight in the eye.

"Why did you come?"

"Do you really have to ask?"

Jessica took a deep breath. "Honestly? I wasn't sure you'd ever speak to me again."

Matt spread his arms wide, a grin on his face, and a look in his eyes that could not be denied.

In spite of everything Jessica had put him through, her stubborn independence, and blatant disregard for danger—even when pointed out with great fervor—he loved her. To his very core, he loved her.

"Oh, Matt."

Matt wrapped his arms around her, and held her close.

"Jessica, you scared me half to death. For three days, I was tormented. Like I told you before you came here, I know how this man thinks, what he's capable of."

After a moment, Matt loosened his grip. He looked down into Jessica's eyes. They shone with tears.

"Did they hurt you?"

Jessica looked away; but Matt gently turned her head back to face him. The slightest touch of his finger on her chin was all it took.

"Not really. I was humiliated, and frightened, and believed they meant to kill me. Mark Huckabee kept saying he knew you sent me. What did he mean by that?"

The door opened again. Special Agent Williams approached them.

"How are you, Miss Roberts? You fell asleep on the way in so we left you in here, where no one could bother you. Until this big lug came along. I hope he didn't wake you."

Jessica's eyes got big.

"It's okay, Jess," said Matt. "Agent Williams and I served together. He's just being a smart aleck."

"That's right," said Agent Williams. "Your friend is a hero. He saved my bacon over there. Snatched me right out of the hands of Mark Huckabee's goons. So, you can imagine what a pleasure it was for me to do the same for you this morning."

Jessica's head began to swim again. The thought of Matt in a war zone, coming against the evil she had just spent three days with, boggled the mind.

It seemed difficult to imagine that the gentle, compassionate, and patient man she knew could be at the helm in the middle of a battle. She couldn't wrap her head around such horror.

"I think I need to sit down," she said.

Matt scrambled to pull up a chair.

"What's happening? Are you in pain?"

Jessica closed her eyes for a moment.

"No, Matt. More like in shock. I'm grateful my traumatic memories are both few and short-lived. How do you deal with the really hard-nosed, bloody, awful memories that must haunt you? Both of you?"

"It's a process," both men said, at once.

"I don't think I've ever said this before, Matt. But thank you for your service to our country. And thank you for flying out here to check on me, in person. I really appreciate it. I appreciate you."

Jessica downed the last of the water. Agent Williams offered her a refill. She nodded, aware for the first time, how blessed she was to simply be alive, and to be loved by a gentle man, a soldier who had willingly risked his life for his country, for his friend.

The room fell silent for a few minutes.

At last, Jessica looked toward Agent Williams. "What happens next? What has happened to Mark Huckabee? Is this ordeal over, or should I expect more trouble down the line?"

Special Agent Williams lowered himself into the chair to Jessica's right. Matt, to her left.

"No one planned for you to be the bait, Miss Roberts."

"Please, call me Jessica."

"Very well. Jessica. We have been after Mark Huckabee for years. The timing of your scheduled interview really was coincidental. The lure turned out to be Matt. Your connection with him drew Mark Huckabee out of hiding. Evidently, he's been keeping an eye on Matt's comings and goings, even after Matt's discharge from the Navy. During interrogation, he confessed to his plan to get back at the United States, and to Matt in particular, for the fall of his empire. After we pulled the plug on him in Afghanistan, he has been struggling to get back to the top of the ladder. Today, he took his final plunge.

"We are truly sorry it took so long to find you. Technology being what it is, we should have been able to locate you on day one; but it didn't happen. Anyway, that's neither here nor there. Huckabee's plan to kill Baldwin and thumb his nose at America did not work. He and his entire crew are in custody. The truth is out about his involvement in Afghanistan and using his corporation to sell arms to the enemy.

"And the good news is, the FBI has agreed to give you an exclusive on the story."

That evening, Matt and Jessica walked down to the wharf, ate out of dough-bowls at a street-side vendor, strolled through the romantic city, just being together and absorbing the cool night air. Peace seemed attainable here, far from the stress of deadlines, and so close to the celebration of life, when a very different ending could have been her reality.

They took pictures with their phones to record this unique and rare evening together. They spoke in hushed tones, and not once did Matt bring up the subject of risk concerning Jessica's job.

Jessica felt a measure of responsibility for the concern she might cause her loved ones to live with, and, without any prompting, promised to make a concerted effort to look at assignments from more than one angle, before plunging headlong into a brood of vipers. And Matt promised to remind her, on occasion, of her promise.

The pain had subsided. The bruises had faded. But the ache in Jessica's heart would take longer to heal. She had survived the greatest threat of her life, and discovered in one look that she owned the heart of a gentle giant. She had a satisfying, albeit challenging, career, and possessed the security of an eternal relationship with her heavenly Father. She could not be more blessed.

But her heart ached for Kimberly. Her best friend lived a lonely life. A confused, scared child, disturbed deep inside by an invisible agony no one else could see. Jessica would return to Lubbock on

Saturday morning. She had made some phone calls and found out that Dirk's trial would begin the following Monday. Excellent. She had not missed it.

Not much time to come up with corroborating witnesses, however. Women who had suffered a similar fate as Kimberly, and would be willing to tell the world. It seemed Kevin Hooper still had not found anyone willing to step forward and testify in court.

Jessica brushed the hair back from her face and turned away from the window, just as a knock sounded at the door.

A smile chased away the gloomy thoughts, for she knew that Matthew Baldwin would be standing on the other side of the door. He had refused to leave her behind; and intended to personally deliver her to her front door. Jessica kept her smile in place as she opened the door, eager to comply.

Chapter 20

Wisdom will save you from the ways of wicked men, from men whose words are perverse, who have left straight paths to walk in dark ways, who delight in doing wrong and rejoice in the perverseness of evil, whose paths are crooked and who are devious in their ways (Proverbs 2:12-15 NIV).

DIRK JOHNSON'S trial began on what otherwise would have been a cheery Monday morning in April—not an ideal way to usher in spring. The accused monster sat smug next to his attorney, grinning as though he had a secret. Jessica glared at him from her seat two rows behind the prosecuting attorney, where she prayed silently, without ceasing. Isn't that what the Bible says in First Thessalonians? Yes, she remembered. They had studied those very verses in Bible study, only yesterday. First Thessalonians 5:16-18: *Rejoice evermore. Pray without ceasing. In everything give thanks: for this is the will of God in Christ Jesus.*

Not all of that passage is easy to comply with, even for a seasoned Christian, thought Jessica. "In everything give thanks," could be a tall order. Today, in the midst of a trial which could go either way, Jessica prayed for strength and mercy, and peace and justice for Kimberly. For that, she could give thanks and rejoice evermore.

But Jessica realized that we are called to obey the Scripture in all things: even if Dirk the Jerk got away with multiple date-rape offenses, God would still expect her family to give thanks. Perhaps thanks that Kimberly had not been killed. Perhaps thanks that she was not with child as a result of the violent attack. Perhaps thanks that Dirk's high-powered, high-paid attorney had not been able to keep his client from going to trial, from facing his latest victim in a court of law—before a jury that would ultimately decide his fate.

"Thank You for all those things," whispered Jessica. "But I'm still asking that justice be served in this regard."

Silently, she continued to pray. *I'm asking for yet another miracle, Lord. I have witnessed Your hand raised against the enemy, and know that nothing escapes Your notice. Not the slightest detail. You see things, know things, that we could not even guess. I'm asking You to reveal all that You know, here, in public, in front of the community that does not know Dirk Johnson III for what he really is. Bring down his reign of terror, manipulation, lies, and abuses. And when it happens, help us give You all the glory.*

Testimonies had been brief by those the prosecuting attorney had called to bring Dirk's true character to light. They testified to much less than they had indicated they might be willing to convey. Jessica remembered being elated when Kevin called to say he had at last found three women who had agreed to testify. To declare themselves as date-rape victims of Dirk Johnson III.

What had happened? Had they been threatened? Could Dirk get to those called to testify against him, even without his father's support? Judge Johnson had chosen not to be in attendance during his son's trial, and refused any statements to the press.

At the close of the day, they weren't much closer to a conviction than when it had begun. As the small crowd filed out of the courthouse, Jessica's cell phone buzzed in her hand, still silent from being turned down during the day's proceedings.

"Excuse me," she said. "I need to get this."

Matt, Kim, Tommy, Catherine, Eunice Mae, and the other Baldwin children made their way to the sidewalk, where they waited for Jessica. A few moments later, Jessica came toward them at a slow jog, a grin plastered across her face, and a light in her eyes.

"You'll never guess who that was!"

"Probably not," said Matt, with a grin. "Why don't you just tell us?"

"Okay, smarty pants," she said, punching Matt in the arm.

"Why do girls do that?"

"Hush," said Jessica, "and listen."

"Sorry. I'm listening."

"We're all listening," said Kim. "What gives?"

"That was Kevin Hooper with the *Avalanche Journal*. Remember, I told you he promised to keep digging?"

"Yes," said Kim. "Did he find something more than we witnessed here today?"

"No, but some<u>body</u> found him. Come on. I told Kevin we'd meet him at Lee's, so he can tell us all about it."

They all climbed into their respective vehicles and headed for Main Street. Jessica jabbered the entire five to seven minutes it took to get to the café. Kevin sounded so positive, like this wasn't some waitress Dirk had been rude to then didn't leave a tip. He indicated this could be a real break for them.

"Please, God, make it so," prayed Jessica, as she stepped out of Matt's rental, and headed for the café entrance.

When they entered the foyer, it only took a moment to spot Kevin seated at a booth in the far-right corner. The judge had dismissed everyone at four o'clock, so they got to the café before the evening rush at five. They moved as one mass to the back corner. Matt took it upon himself to pull two other tables together so they could all sit close by and hear the news as a group.

The report was put on hold just long enough for each of them to place their order. But the second that chore was done, Jessica urged Kevin to tell them what in the world was going on. What news was so big he hadn't wanted to share it over the phone?

Come Wednesday morning, following Christopher's approval from Judge Samuels to continue testimony on behalf of the prosecution, the bailiff called Allison McNew to the stand.

Jessica watched Dirk to see if he reacted to the name. Nothing. He didn't raise an eyebrow, or turn to look when she came up the aisle right next to him, on her way to the witness stand.

Jessica listened while Allison was sworn in, but kept glancing toward Dirk Johnson. Apparently, he had no clue what was coming.

Good.

Allison McNew stated her name and promised to tell the truth.

She looked over at Dirk only once, for a brief moment. Seeing him there, at the mercy of the law, warmed her heart. He was about to be exposed in a big way.

Christopher Watson, the prosecuting attorney, addressed her, asked if she was ready and willing to testify on behalf of the prosecution.

"Yes, sir."

Allison sat tall and straight in her seat. No trace of humiliation or shame. Her shoulders did not hunch over as they had done for months after her initial encounter with Dirk Johnson. Today, she would let him see the woman she had become, despite his cruelty.

"You have the floor," said Christopher Watson.

Allison took a deep breath, sat up even taller in her seat and told her story. She did not falter, or break down, or hesitate. She told the whole truth, and left nothing for the jury to wonder about.

She introduced her daughter, who stood at the back of the room when her mother explained who had fathered her then deserted her, before she was born. Gasps could be heard all over the room, for Summer's resemblance to Dirk Johnson proved to be nothing less than miraculous. An uncanny replica of the man on trial.

She revealed the mockery she had endured by Dirk Johnson and his father. She spoke of the months and years she had struggled on her own. But she also gave credit to a merciful God who had provided bus fare through a local church so she could relocate to Tennessee, where she worked a full-time job until her baby came in August. She bragged on Jesus for encouraging a wonderful group of ladies affiliated with a ministry that pooled its resources to house Allison and her baby. They provided loving, Christian day care for little Summer so her mother could work and go back to school.

"I now have my own practice in Nashville," said Allison. "A firm that represents both established and aspiring artists in the field of music. God has taken something meant for evil, and made it something good and beautiful.

"I will never be sorry that Summer is my daughter, Dirk," she said, turning to face the defendant one last time. "But I am extremely grateful to be part of these proceedings today, so I can be present when the sentencing comes down. May God have mercy on your soul, in accordance with His will."

Judge Samuels looked toward Dirk's attorney. "Do you have any questions for this witness?"

"No questions, Your Honor. The defense rests."

"The defense rests?" cried Dirk. "What makes you think she's not lying through her teeth? I don't even remember her. Now, get up there and do your job. Defend me."

The D.A. stood and addressed the judge.

"A five-minute break, Your Honor?"

Judge Samuels rapped the gavel twice.

"We will break for fifteen minutes. Get your client under control, Counselor. Ms. McNew, you may step down."

Fifteen minutes didn't change anything for Dirk Johnson. Court resumed right on time. The judge allowed the signed and notarized affidavits that Allison had brought with her as further evidence of Dirk's long history of manipulation and abuse, in the form of multiple sworn statements from girls who had been afraid to face him in court. A total of 20 women had signed their name before a notary public in order to see Dirk Johnson brought to justice. Twenty women, eight of whom had put themselves through the eternal agony of abortion. Half of them admitted to dating Dirk several times before he drugged them and had his way with them. They had been driven home in tears, pushed out at the curb, and never called again. Just like Kimberly Baldwin.

The jury deliberated for all of forty-five minutes. Guilty. Dirk Johnson III had been found guilty of rape.

Sentencing followed one week later. As the Baldwin family sat linked hand in hand, the judge pronounced the sentence. The maximum of twenty years, when the date-rape drug was involved, rang through the courthouse. The bang of the gavel echoed across the room, barely audible above the roar of celebratory shouts.

With tears spilling out on her cheeks, Kimberly approached Allison and her beautiful daughter.

"I can't thank you enough."

Allison reached out and gave Kim a squeeze. "No, I can't thank you enough. I've waited years for someone to be brave enough to press charges against Dirk. And I want you to know, it's not over. Now that we have this conviction under our belts, I have a feeling that a lot of the women who signed affidavits will be willing to press charges against the snake, too. And I intend to do the same. He won't be hurting anyone else, hopefully, ever again."

Kimberly couldn't contain herself. The tears flowed freely, gratefully, as she realized Dirk Johnson would be facing multiple counts of rape charges.

Jessica put an arm across Kim's shoulders and reached the other one out to Allison. "Thank you so much."

"My pleasure," said Allison. "Thank all of you. And just so you know, in most cases where the perpetrator is guilty of more than one offense, and especially in light of the fact that Dirk drugged his victims, the maximum penalty automatically doubles, which would mean forty years, per each of these next cases that is filed and heard, and for which he is convicted. It's a beautiful day in the neighborhood, my new friends."

Allison and Summer returned to Nashville the day after Judge Samuels pronounced sentencing over Dirk Johnson III. A sunny, warm Friday. The following Sunday, Allison smiled, gratified, when she read the latest article in regard to Dirk's trial.

Just as she reached the end of the article, someone knocked on the front door.

"I'll get it, Mom," said Summer.

"Is Allison home?"

"Yes, sir."

"May I see her, please?"

"I guess so. Mom, it's for you."

Allison came around the corner, the newspaper still in her hand. When she saw the tall, gray-haired man standing in her doorway, the newspaper fell to the floor and sent sections of it scooting across the parquet flooring.

"Judge Johnson."

"Yes, ma'am. Sorry to bother you on a Sunday, but could we talk?"

Summer gathered up the newspaper and moved toward the den.

"Please stay," said Judge Johnson. "This concerns you, too."

"Mom?"

"It's okay, sweetie. Let's move into the den."

Something in his eyes told Allison she was looking at a changed man. Kindness, compassion, and sorrow looked back at her, mingled with what appeared to be a measure of guilt and remorse.

"Can I offer you anything, Judge Johnson?"

"Maybe later, if this goes well. And please, call me Dewayne, my middle name."

Allison sat mesmerized, her hand clinging to Summer's, as Judge Johnson spilled his heart out to them. He apologized profusely for the atrocious way she had been treated by him and his family. He gushed with heartache as he tried to explain trying to raise his son alone, a widower since Dirk had been five years old. He wept at all the times he had come to the aid of his son, believing his lies, and falling victim to his son's practiced manipulation.

"Anyway," said Judge Johnson, wiping tears from his cheeks with the tissue Summer had offered him. "I came here to beg your forgiveness, and to ask a huge favor."

"What favor, Judge. I mean, Dewayne?"

"Could you bring yourself to allow me to be Summer's grandfather? In a real way? She is the only grandchild I know anything about. The only grandchild I may ever know. I would like to try and make up for the past, and share the future with the two of you."

Summer began to cry.

"Well, what do you think, Summer?" said Allison.

Summer looked at her mother, smiled through her tears, released her fingers from Allison's grasp, and stood. She took one step toward her grandfather.

That was all the answer he needed. Judge Dirk Dewayne Johnson, Jr. stood and hurried to meet his granddaughter in the middle of the room, where she had lived in obscurity, lo these many years. His heart burst with joy. He didn't bother wiping away the tears, just let them fall, making Summer's hair damp as she placed her head against his chest.

"Thank You, God," he whispered.

"Yes, thank You, God," whispered Allison.

Chapter 21

In their hearts humans plan their course, but the LORD establishes their steps. (Proverbs 16:9 NIV).

MID-MAY, article five on the life of Eunice Mae Howell hit the stands.

As Matt read the announcement, his mind began to churn. He set the magazine to one side and picked up his phone. Speed dial would work well for him today.

He called Brooke first then Kim immediately after, for they were considered the family planners. They would be able to best assist him with such a large endeavor. He called Paul and James to make sure everyone would be in total agreement. The girls would handle Grandmother Baldwin, the flowers, the limo, and the food. His job would be to get flight connections for everyone, and arrange transportation from the airport. There would be no stand-by flights for this occasion. He didn't want to take a chance on anyone missing out. And, of course, he would need to arrange for time off and permission to escort Jessica and Eunice Mae to the WASP homecoming festivities. Now that the chaos Dirk Johnson's trial had stirred up was behind them, the entire family could be present at the WASP homecoming reunion.

Article Five

I have been chosen to give homage to the heroic ladies of WASP by filling my allotted space with pictures. Pictures that depict the struggles they endured and the victories that had been swept under the rug, even as lives had been saved by their willingness to serve—and as many of them lost their own.

I spoke with several family members who had lost a sweetheart, a daughter, or an aunt to the war effort. These dear people are very proud of the legacy the WASP pilots left in their wake. I spoke with females who grabbed hold of the memories and shaped a future of their own—unafraid to take a chance. Bold in their endeavors, they looked challenges in the face, and beat them back, overcame, and persevered.

It is with great honor that I invite you to join in the celebration of those who served to keep our country free. And especially invite you to buy a ticket for the banquet, and hear Ms. Eunice Mae's story—in person.

Eunice Mae had taken her time as she strolled through the displays. She read every word beneath every picture. She watched every minute of available footage, and listened to every word of every documentary and personal testimony, including her own. She stared in amazement at the beautiful job that had been done with her own personal information and collection of photos. She wept openly before the pictures of the women she had served with, who had passed away—both during the war, and the years that followed.

Eunice Mae dressed in a replica of the WASP pilot uniform she had worn during the war, except for the fact that this one had been tailored to better fit her physique. The clothing they had been issued back in the day had been notoriously ill-fitting.

Ninety-two, notwithstanding, Eunice Mae stood to her feet without assistance, approached the podium with dignity and moist eyes. Her face shown like an angel, and she told her story to an enthralled crowd, much as she had told it to me.

A sea of people had come to honor the WASP pilots Eunice Mae had served with. Not one person from her extended family came from Atlanta to share in the reunion; but the sting had long gone out of that bite. Her true family filled two tables at the banquet.

I sat near the center of the aisle, camera at the ready. I had already taken a myriad of photographs throughout the chilly, damp, windy day. An unusual forecast for West Texas had proven to be on-point. The vintage plane flights had been delayed because of the weather, but that disappointment proved to be a minor one, considering the band of citizens who had rallied in support of this memorable event.

Eunice Mae Howell admitted to me that she would be physically exhausted and emotionally spent the next day—but at the moment, she couldn't care *less. She could have gone on to glory that day, satisfied that the sacrifices the WASP pilots had made at last had been celebrated, recognized, appreciated.*

I felt tears trail down my face as I listened with pride to the bold, brave, heroic lady I have learned to admire and adore.

Eunice Mae let her eyes drift from face to face throughout the dining hall. She took in every detail of the room, and grinned from ear to ear. Yes, this day, this evening, this milestone would be forever burned in her heart. Even if she went home to be with the Lord today, or tomorrow, that would be okay. She had lived a long, full, adventurous life, and did not take lightly any moment of it. Her heart swelled with the many times she had been reckless with her own life, and God had rescued her in the midst of her foolishness. God had sent dear people into her life to cushion the sting of loss and keep love alive. When she stood before Him in Glory, she fully expected to hear, "This one is Mine. I know her by name."

Slowly, one person at a time, those in attendance rose to their feet and began to applaud—and Eunice Mae had not yet said a single word. Tears spilled over on her cheeks, and Eunice Mae let them fall. She realized these kind and grateful people were not standing to honor her alone; but were demonstrating a great measure of respect for what all the WASP pilots had stood for, all they had accomplished—against great odds.

Momentarily, Eunice Mae joined in the applause, and wept for all those who could not be here to witness such a grand outpouring of gratitude.

Still further, the family stayed in Lubbock overnight. They crowded into Trinity Church for services the following day. They moved together to Abuelo's after church to have lunch, and didn't care a whit about the wait. They each had their own set of special memories with Eunice Mae, and intended to show her how much they loved and admired her, every moment a treasure they would hold in their hearts long after they parted ways. Long after they had stepped into eternity.

Chapter 22

He takes no pleasure in the strength of a horse or in human might. No, the LORD's delight is in those who fear him, those who put their hope in his unfailing love (Psalm 147:10-11 NLT).

JESSICA spotted Heather Jackson at the airport. Her head told her what a great reporter she was being; but her heart had mixed emotions about this unplanned, unreported, untoward adventure. She knew Matt would be beside himself with worry when the news broke. The timing of her departure, her secrecy, and the disappearance of the daughter of the Vice President of the United States of America, would all be a little too coincidental to be considered a coincidence.

And it wasn't such a coincidence, after all. It was a miraculous turn of events that had put Jessica Roberts in the right place at the right time.

Georgianna served as live-in housekeeper for the family of the Vice President, just as she had the previous Vice President, and the Vice President before that.

Heather Jackson escaped out her bedroom window at two in the morning; and Jessica had signed off on her latest assignment, in D.C., at one o'clock that same morning. Seconds before Jessica was ready to don her pajamas, Georgianna called. She had seen Heather sneak out in the dead of night, and had almost run into her as she came around the corner of the house with every intention of stopping Heather's escape.

Georgianna had been feeding Jessica tidbits from the Vice President's dining room for going on six months now. Georgianna had said Jessica Roberts was the first, and only, white woman to stay for dinner at the Vice President's home, and not just speak to her, but actually ask her name, where she came from, and also thanked her for keeping the restroom so nice and clean. They'd met after her interview with George Jackson, the Vice President. Jessica had left her business card with Georgianna, and they'd been communicating every few weeks since.

"But I couldn't tell on her, Jess. You should have seen the pleading in those big blue eyes. I just couldn't do it. But I can tell you what she's wearing. I can describe the backpack she's carrying, and I can definitely tell you the information on her boarding pass, which I spotted earlier in the day, when I was straightening up in her room. I fear she is going to meet a boy, Jessica. But I don't know who, and

I don't know if Mr. Jackson would approve of him. Please get to her and bring her back, Miss Jessica. Please."

Jessica soothed Georgianna as best she could, disconnected the call, then grabbed her "go luggage" and her equipment bag, and raced out the door, headed for the Ronald Reagan International Airport.

Heather was seated in a chair outside Gate 37. The hood of her jacket was pulled up over her flaxen blond hair, and she wore dark glasses to cover her eyes. But Heather's inside information made the identification unmistakable. And the information on the boarding pass had made knowing what ticket to purchase, a synch.

Jessica tucked her own boarding pass in the outside pocket of her backpack, and settled in one seat down and behind Heather Jackson, waiting, watching for a sign, or a move, or an attack. Some hint to explain Heather's clandestine escape from her father's home.

What Jessica saw surprised her more than if a terrorist had held Heather at gunpoint.

Heather Jackson had escaped to meet a boy, all right. But not just any boy. This boy happened to be the son of the Secretary of the Navy! The boy, Jake, she thought, arrived about ten minutes after Jessica. She saw him standing across the room, searching the few faces that waited for the red-eye flight. She made eye contact with him briefly, but looked away, aware that he was moving toward her. He was cute, with curly black hair and ice blue eyes, tall and broad-shouldered. Definitely familiar with a workout routine, but still very young. She guessed him to be two or three years older than Heather. Jessica did not wish him to think her glance his way could be construed as interest. When she chanced another look toward Heather, Jessica about came up out of her seat. This handsome young man sat himself down next to the daughter of the Vice President of the United States of America. She did not flinch, but had a broad grin on her face. Jake, if that was his name, lifted Heather's hand and kissed the back side of it. She smiled at him, as a single tear slipped down her face.

So, little Heather has a boyfriend. Did they really have to escape to another country in order to see one another? And all the way to Jamaica? Their little tryst could cause an international incident!

Well, Jessica didn't know, but she was sticking around to find out exactly what these kids were up to, and do her level best to talk Heather Jackson into voluntarily returning to her father's home. Before the strength of the White House discovered where Heather had gone. And before the bad guys of the world discovered the opportunity to hold hostage a treasure of a high political official. If this turned into a terrorist situation, a pleasant secret trip to Jamaica could turn sour in a hurry.

Lord, please send angels to watch over us, and give me an opportunity to talk straight to Heather Jackson. She obviously has no idea what a delicate position she has put herself in.

The boarding numbers were called, and the passengers lined up to present their boarding passes. Jessica kept one eye on her own boarding pass, and one eye on the unsuspecting happy couple.

Matt Baldwin listened to his voicemails again, hoping against hope that he'd heard wrong. But Jessica's voice still sounded the same, excited, pumped, the voice of a big story just waiting for her. The voice that spelled danger for her, and lots of knee time, for him.

"O, Jess, what are you doing? Where are you going? How much danger are you walking into?"

Matt didn't hesitate. He called Jessica's mother, and then his own. Knowing those two, everyone in the family, and more, would soon be praying for Jessica Roberts.

The red-eye flight was only half full, so Jessica managed to sit where she could see Heather and Jake through the slight opening between the seats in front of her. While Jessica fought sleep, the runaways held hands, stared into each other's eyes, and talked, and talked, and talked.

And Jessica let them. At long last, she decided to take a nap. It would be at least a couple hours before they reached Fort Lauderdale, where they would change planes and head for Kingston, Jamaica. The "kids" wouldn't be going anywhere before then. Maybe after a nap,

Jessica would be better able to keep up with Heather, and figure out some way to approach her without spooking her. Kingston, Jamaica was a tangled maze, and Jessica did not want to lose her "charge."

When Matthew Baldwin opened the *Dallas Morning News* on Friday morning, the truth slammed into him. Suddenly, Jessica's, "This could be the biggest story of my career," took on a whole new meaning. Instinct, and a little history with Jessica Roberts, told him that Jessica had gone in search of Heather Jackson. His heart sank. Heather's disappearance received national, and international, coverage. The whole world would know. And the whole world didn't have Heather's best interests in mind. Or Jessica's, for that matter.

At the Fort Lauderdale airport, Jessica had managed to sit close enough to Heather to overhear where the couple would be staying as John and Jane Smith. Not very original, but it probably would not shock any host in any hotel or remote cabin near Kingston. And Heather might not be readily recognized in Jamaica. She had to give these two some credit. They had made a plan; and it seemed to be working for them.

Right then, Jessica left her seat and moved away from Heather, where she could have a private telephone conversation. She got busy on the phone, and booked a cabin two doors down from the kids who wanted to be treated like adults. She could have hugged them both for not running away at the height of tourist season. Otherwise, booking a cabin on such short notice would have been impossible. And to snag a cabin two doors down was nothing short of a miracle. But then, Jessica had grown, more and more, to expect miracles on a daily basis.

Jessica hoped to befriend Heather and her companion, before they managed to get married, or slip off into the night again. This time, there would be no Georgianna to tattle on them. Jessica whispered a quick prayer for Georgianna. Turning her face away as the Vice President's daughter snuck out of the house could very well cost her, her job. A job no level-headed, self-respecting politician would offer her a second chance at, no matter how pitiful Heather Jackson had appeared the night of her getaway. No matter how many vice presidents Georgianna had worked for.

But like most reporters, Jessica was determined to protect the identity of her source. Hopefully, the Secret Service would not torture the information out of her.

With getting acquainted in mind, Jessica passed by Heather and company, on the way to the restroom on board the aircraft. No eye contact, no exchange, just walked by them like any normal person might do.

On the way back, however, Jessica caught her toe on the outside edge of the cute guy's shoe and almost tumbled onto his lap.

"Oh!" cried Jessica. "I'm so sorry. I didn't notice where I was stepping."

"It's okay," said Heather.

The catch in Heather's voice, like she'd been crying, alarmed Jessica. She looked straight into the young girl's eyes. And she knew. Something had gone terribly wrong with their plan.

The Lord must have sent at least one angel ahead to make a way, because Heather and her companion were seated in the two seats up front that put their backs to the rest of the passengers, and the two seats across from them had remained empty. Perhaps because the young man had long legs and stretched them out underneath the other two seats. Or maybe because an angel had been guarding it for Jessica's use. She didn't ask if she could sit down; she just did—directly across from Heather Jackson.

"Heather, my name is Jessica Roberts. I'm."

"I know who you are," said Heather. "I saw you at the airport. And now I have to ask, Have you exposed me?"

"No," said Jessica, just above a whisper. Being overheard at this juncture would not help anyone. "Absolutely not. I need to know why you're upset though. Has something happened to frighten you?"

Heather didn't say a word, just stretched out her hand, and presented the now-crumpled note over to her.

"I hope you're telling the truth. I have to trust someone."

Jessica opened the note and read it quickly: *I know who you are. If you are smart you will surrender yourself to me as soon as we disembark. If you cooperate you will not be harmed.*

"Come with me," said Jessica. She stood and looked over the rest of the passengers. No one seemed to be watching them at the moment. Jessica took Heather by the hand and led her around the corner into the front restroom. They both squeezed in and talked as the roar of the vent muffled their voices.

"Okay," said Jessica. "Tell me who and when."

Heather sniffed and pressed the tears off her face with her palms. A few seconds passed before she could speak.

"I was coming out of the ladies' room at the airport in Fort Lauderdale when a man bumped into me. He apologized and moved on. When I got back to my seat I found this note in my pocket. Oh, what am I going to do? Daddy will be so mad."

"He's more scared than mad right now, I imagine," said Jessica. "Is the man who bumped into you on this plane?"

'Yes. All the way in the back. Blue pin-striped suit. Looks like a businessman, not a tourist or a terrorist. I'm scared, Miss Roberts. I've never been so scared."

Someone knocked on the door.

Heather's eyes got big.

"Don't worry. I don't think he'll try anything on the plane."

Jessica reached around Heather and opened the door. A flight attendant stood on the other side.

"We've had several requests to see if everything is all right in here. And we need the facility to be available. You understand, I'm sure."

Heather stepped out. Jessica followed.

"We understand," said Jessica. "Sorry. Just needed a short, private conversation."

"Thank you for your cooperation."

Heather sat beside her travelling companion. Jessica returned to her original seat just long enough to retrieve her backpack then made her way up front, to join Heather and, was it Jake? She needed to remember to ask.

When Jessica sat down across from Heather, she made a point to use a normal tone of voice, emphasizing how wonderfully coincidental it had been to run into Heather so far away from home.

"And who is your friend? I don't believe we've met."

Heather looked over at her traveling companion and raised a questioning brow. He offered his hand in greeting to Jessica. "Jake Torrey," he said. "Get Heather out of this safely, and my family will reward you handsomely."

"I thought that's who you were, just wanted to make sure. And I'll do my best to get Heather out of this safely, regardless. I'd really love to know how this all came about. But right now, I need to get busy. There are a few discreet people with power that I can contact in Miami, who should be more than willing to meet our plane in Kingston, and be ready to nab your not-so-friendly would-be captor.

You two carry on, pretend I'm not here, and when this is all settled maybe we can have dinner, and you can tell me all about it."

Jessica was fully aware that Miami, Florida was the twin city to Kingston, Jamaica. They supported each other, promoted each other, and she felt certain would be willing to come to political aid for each other. She prayed so, anyway.

As Heather and Jake whispered and consoled one another, Jessica did what Jessica did best. She used her contacts to bring together the officials in Kingston and the officials in Miami. She sent an email to the Vice President, assuring him that his daughter was safe. Then later passed on to the White House, the proposed plan of attack and apprehension, upon arrival in Kingston.

Once Jessica believed she had done everything within her means to insure Heather's safety, and Jake's absolution, she sent an email to Matt:

> *You have probably guessed by now, but I got a tip and followed Heather Jackson out of D.C. We are merrily on our way to Kingston, Jamaica. All is well. The matter will be resolved upon landing. There is much to tell, and I'll catch you up when I get back. Sorry about the short, abrupt notice, but time was of the essence.*

Much love, Jess.

Matt Baldwin read the email again. It took a minute to absorb the fact that he had been right about where Jessica may have wandered off to. That she was actually with Heather Jackson, and had already made arrangements for her safe return. Crazy. But great. He could breathe again. For now.

"Thank You, Lord. But please don't let up. This thing may not come off as smoothly as Jessica would like to believe."

Matt had warned her that her plan could go wrong in so many ways; and he'd been right. Once the plane landed at Norman Manley International Airport, Jessica made a point to stay between Heather and the businessman. Apprehension should have been a breeze. But the businessman had not come alone.

Within seconds after Heather, Jake, and Jessica stepped into the terminal, businessman pushed Jessica to one side and yanked Heather toward him by the hood of her jacket. Heather screamed.

Businessman had a large companion who blocked Jake from being able to get to Heather. But once they had pushed Jessica to the side, they dismissed her. Big mistake. She ran straight toward the contact she'd made in Miami.

"Don't worry, Miss Roberts," he said. "These clowns are not just up against airport security. There are several CIA agents in this room, making their way toward them, as we speak, and several Secret Service men are right behind them."

It was over in what seemed like an eternity to Jessica, but had only amounted to a few minutes. Once the businessman and his colleague were in custody, Jessica ran toward Heather. A member of Secret Service held an arm out to keep her from getting too close.

"It's okay," said Heather. "This is Jessica Roberts. She saved us."

Although the Vice President was more than anxious to have his daughter returned home immediately, he agreed to let Heather stay over one night, under very heavy, and close, guard in order to tell her story. Yes, Jessica Roberts would be granted exclusive coverage. After all, without this stubborn reporter's tenacity, all of D.C. shuddered at what might have become the fate of George Jackson's daughter and her heartthrob, Jake Torrey. And no, Jake Torrey could not stay. He was ordered, in no uncertain terms, to return home on the next available flight. CIA would travel with him; then he would face his father in D.C.

Jessica watched a tearful farewell as Jake boarded the airplane to start the journey home. It was the right thing to do. Their relationship would have to be negotiated, no doubt, but Jessica believed it could be worked out to everyone's satisfaction. Heather, Jessica knew, would turn eighteen the following March, so if a relationship with Jake was meant to be, it could wait that long, at least.

Heather stayed in the original cabin she had booked in advance, surrounded by CIA and Secret Service, and Jessica stayed two doors down. But that evening, and into the early hours of the morning, Jessica got the scoop on Heather Jackson, her home life, and the love of her life, Jake Torrey.

Mutual trust can grow a friendship at warp speed. The two of them discovered that they shared photography as a common passion. Jessica encouraged Heather to stand up to her father's dream for her to become an attorney and to pursue her true dream to one day be a world-renowned photographer.

Heather had been following Jessica's articles on Eunice Mae Howell, and didn't take much convincing that a woman had a right to chase her dreams, and still have a personal life. In fact, Eunice Mae's story had given Heather the idea to take matters into her own hands, and force her father to accept, and respect, Heather's life choices.

But Eunice Mae had put her foot down in order to come to the aid of her country during a time of war. Heather's rebellion had been thwarted by a political agenda Heather could not control, on a whim. Even so, Jessica believed everything would work out in the end.

Chapter 23

My victory and honor come from God alone. He is my refuge, a rock where no enemy can reach me (Psalm 62:7 NLT).

THE WIND blew. Branches scraped across the cracked and dirty windows, as rain dripped incessantly in one corner, off the edge of the dresser, and sprayed a fine mist on everything within reach. Jessica had been in Jamaica on assignment for five long days. Heather Jackson had been escorted safely home. Jessica Roberts had retained her cabin long enough to write the story, and carefully maintain her integrity as a reporter. Although Jessica had not encouraged Heather to sneak out of her home to meet a boy, and run off to Jamaica, she had had a source whom she refused to reveal. There could very well be major, unpleasant repercussions for her actions. All she could do was hope and pray for God's grace and mercy. She had, after all, diffused a potentially disastrous situation. Surely, everyone could tell that, anyway. Surely.

Jessica could face the Vice President of the United States, without much of a tremor. Facing Matt, however, concerned her a bit. In his latest email, Matt had made it plain that these lengthy, overseas, potentially dangerous assignments made him uneasy. After the incident with Mark Huckabee, Jessica had almost agreed with him. Right up to the moment she'd receive the tip about Heather. She had taken off, with just a short voicemail to Matt. She had been unwilling to go through another hour-long discussion about her safety. She left, not really knowing what she might be up against.

What if Heather had been discovered, and kidnapped, or killed? What if Jessica and Heather had both been in danger? Danger they could not escape. So many what-ifs. No wonder Matthew had called early on to express his concern. No wonder he thought Jessica should just call the White House and turn the whole thing over to the Secret Service.

Jessica had put herself in dangerous circumstances, on more than one occasion, because she wanted a story.

Once Heather had been reunited with her family and the truth came out, even Eunice Mae had sent an e-mail expressing her concern for Jessica's rash decision to trail off after a wayward daughter without clearance from the White House, or knowing what she might be walking into.

The e-mail had been sobering. Maybe it was time for her to check her priorities. Did she want to damage treasured relationships for the sake of a story? Even Eunice Mae Howell, the greatest adventurer Jessica had ever known, had managed to balance her love of flying with a beautiful romance, and had suggested Jessica pray about the life she really wanted. Pray about balance, and love, and life, and pleasing God.

Yes, her career as an independent photo journalist had taken off. She made decent money—and paid the high price of weeks and months without family or a familiar face with which to converse. She was beginning to understand what Eunice Mae had said about balancing your adventures with a personal life. A committed relationship that included another human being, and respecting his desires and expectations. Jessica was beginning to believe there was more to life than work and travel.

The howl of the tropical storm reminded her just how homesick she could get.

She'd been bitten, it would seem, by an adventure bug the day she'd arrived on this surly planet. And part of her longed to see every nook and cranny of it. For the past three years, she had checked off country after country, until she felt a need to stay in the States for a while and explore each state from border to border, north, south, east and west.

A crack of thunder and flickering lights set her to praying the storm would soon pass, so she could make her flight, scheduled to leave in the late afternoon on the following day. In an attempt to hasten its arrival, Jessica donned her night clothes, brushed her teeth, turned out the lights, closed the mosquito net about the bed, and squeezed her eyes shut. She drifted off to sleep in the middle of a prayer.

Morning greeted Jessica as the blessed rays of sunshine flooded her room. She stretched and yawned, grateful for the break in the weather. Her bed had remained dry; perhaps the patch job on the roof had actually worked. The manager of the facility had been kind and compassionate.

Jessica clambered quickly out of bed, with hope in her heart.

Dressed and groomed, Jessica set about tidying the room and packing her things. She whistled a tune she had learned from a local fisherman, down by the river, where she preferred to write...

Jessica stood barefoot at the rocky edge of the water, and waved at Serek as he floated by in his low-to-the-water, practically flat boat, which he used to show tourists the breathtaking landscape of Jamaica. She had met Serek herself on such a tour. The two tourists he had with him today waved back at Jessica. She smiled as she watched Serek glide smoothly through water, until he made the bend in the river, and she could no longer see him.

Jessica sipped from the bottled water she found so precious then returned to the chaise lounge that had been provided with the cabin.

She settled in, picked up her laptop, and smiled as she absorbed the perfect temperature, listened for the ever-present bird calls, and let the soothing lap, lap, lap of the water calm her soul. She may have to face some stuff when she got home, but no one could take her memories. The memory of a long night talking with Heather Jackson, getting to know her hopes and dreams. Just being an ear.

The night before, Jessica had received a telegram from George Jackson: *All calm on the western front.* STOP *All is forgiven.* STOP *Please join us, by invitation of the President, to a gala held in honor of Heather's safe return.* STOP *Bring a date if you'd like.* STOP.

Maybe going home would not be so bad, after all.

Yes, sir, today would be a good day. She could feel it in her soul. The story had been completed and submitted. Jessica had found peace in Jamaica.

An unexpected knock on the door drew Jessica back to the moment. She crossed the room and opened the door, curious who might still be in town, and would care to speak to her. All the other news crews had left the area. The excitement, over. The story, told.

Her brows raised in genuine surprise as Jessica looked up into the face of Matthew Baldwin, grinning his signature grin, and holding his pilot cap under his left arm.

"Matt," she whispered, unable to say more.

"Yes," he said with a laugh. "You look surprised."

"Should I have been expecting you?"

"No, I guess you couldn't be. I've come to rescue you, and forgot to wire ahead."

Rescue me?

Jessica Roberts had fallen hard for Matthew Baldwin; then spent the next two years running in the opposite direction. Afraid that he was afraid of commitment. Afraid he might expect more from her than she could give. Afraid she would have to sacrifice adventure for the mundane. Matt had never, as far as anyone knew, had a serious girlfriend before her. That scared Jessica. She did not want to end up a blubbering statistic, with Matt walking away into the sunset, with another girl on his arm. And not even looking back.

"Rescue me?" she said aloud. "From what, exactly?"

"I read the newspapers, Jess."

"Oh. Sorry. Come in. Excuse my manners."

It wasn't true. None of it was true. The newspapers had made it sound like half the world was on Jessica's trail. That half the bad guys who hated the United States of America had sent people out to intercept the return of the Vice President's daughter. But Jessica had not seen anyone even tailing her. No one without credentials had approached her. No one had threatened her life, or interfered with Heather's return to her father, safely guarded, once again, by the Secret Service. Heather was fine. Jessica was fine. Matthew really had not needed to make the trip.

Jessica noticed Matt looking around the room.

"Sorry again. I have stuff scattered everywhere."

"I'm good with standing. Are you about packed? I thought we could grab a bite then head for the airport. Your life could be in danger, and I'm not letting you out of my sight until you are safely in your living room. I brought my own plane, hoping you would let me take you home."

He grinned again, and Jessica could not resist his offer. It was so like him to come to the rescue. He had shown up when there had really been a threat. He had shown up after Afghanistan. He had shown up at every possible opportunity. She knew she could trust him. Knew he loved her. Yes, she would go with him, and gladly. She didn't much think her life was in danger. An investigation was still under way, but it appeared that businessman and his thug acted alone. Right place, right time. Heather Jackson, traveling without a single Secret Service escort, had been more than the two low-lifes could resist. Their dream of millions of dollars in ransom money had been quashed before it got much of a start.

"I'm mostly packed," said Jessica. "Won't take me but a minute to finish."

Matt leaned forward, placed his cap back on his head and his right hand on the door facing, inching closer to her face, until they stood eyeball to eyeball.

"Okay," she said. "I'm coming."

"A kiss hello?"

But he didn't wait for an answer.

Jessica thought she must look silly, as he pulled away. She hadn't moved, hadn't opened her eyes. No one had ever kissed her like Matt. Or made her swoon like Matt. Or scared her like Matt.

His laughter shook her, and she turned crimson.

"Come on," he said. "I'll help you carry stuff."

Jessica followed Matt to the airport, where she turned in the car she had rented two weeks earlier. As she stepped inside his plane, Matt simply squeezed her shoulder then moved to the cockpit. She smiled up at him.

The compact Lear jet made her smile. Leather seats, a screen to follow their airborne progress, a single attendant, and they seemed to have on board, anything she might ask for. A Lear jet of his own. Matthew Baldwin had been holding out on her.

But Jessica didn't linger on any questions or try to figure out what might come next. She simply closed her eyes and slept—peacefully, serenely, and better than she had in months.

Three Weeks Later

Matt had agreed to go to the Vice President's celebration; and Jessica had begged Kimberly to tag along with her and Eunice Mae when they went shopping for what a regular person might wear to a party at the White House. The result pleased Kimberly and Eunice

Mae alike, and they wholeheartedly agreed that the overall effect would more than please Matt.

Jessica stood in front of the full-length mirror, and could scarcely believe her eyes. Her blonde hair, cut in a long version of a swing, freshly highlighted, shown in the light of the chandelier that graced her hotel room. She smiled into a face more made-up than it had been in years. Maybe ever.

Kim had raved over the shimmering polished-cotton lime green gown. It fit Jessica in all the right places, and was draped with a long sash that rested across her throat and hung a short way down her back. The sleeves were slender at the waist and followed the line of her arm, up to her shoulder, not too tight, or too poofy. It was just right.

Kim had hired a professional to do Jessica's hair and makeup, a thank-you for her part in bringing home the Vice President's daughter, and an overdue thank-you for her support and research, and unwavering friendship before, during and after Dirk Johnson's trial.

During those awful days when Heather had been missing, it didn't matter what political party her father represented—the entire country had rallied around him. How often, really, does the daughter of a high political official escape her home in the middle of the night, and manage to get on a plane bound for Jamaica, without being kidnapped by some terrorist group—then come back with nothing more than remorse and guilt for injuries?

Kim had insisted Jessica be treated like the celebrity she had become—practically overnight. Brave, undaunted, bold, and determined to follow every lead until Heather could be reunited with her parents, Jessica had amazed every journalist in the country. And, she learned later, scared the pants off every member of her family, as well as Kim's family.

Once the truth came out, Jessica soon learned that the Vice President doubled the security detail around his daughter, grounded her for a month—and confiscated her laptop and cell phone. She would not be agreeing to meet a boy (any boy, no matter who his father happened to be) anytime in the near future. Her father had been terrified—and livid. The negotiations for Heather's impending relationship would be considered after her eighteenth birthday. Her tears had not swayed her father. She would suffer the consequences of her actions.

A knock at the door.

Jessica froze for a moment, staring at her reflection; then laughed at herself, shrugged her shoulders, and turned the light off in the dressing area. She felt silly, really; the girly side of her didn't surface too often. And she had never dressed this elaborately, or allowed some stranger to do her hair and makeup. Oh well, it would just be for one night. She could handle it for one night. Then on Monday morning, she would be herself again. The coach would be a pumpkin again, and the footman would be a horse. She determined in her heart to keep her wits about her, and get home with both of her shoes.

Jessica had seen Matt in a tux before. She had seen him in uniform as a commercial airline pilot, and had seen pictures of him in his dress blue Navy uniform. But when the door to her suite swung open, and she saw him on this special night, her heart leapt into her throat, and she knew, without a doubt, she was addicted. In that moment, she knew the answer to the question in the letter she had received long ago. The letter she still carried in her purse. The letter she had not answered.

Dear God, save this man for me. Forgive my doubt, and my selfish ambition. Please, Sir, give me a chance, an opportunity, to say yes.

Epilogue

"You do realize you've married a photo journalist, right?"

Matt laughed. "A deeply entrenched one," he said. "Yes, I do. And I wouldn't change one single thing about her. Not even that."

Matt crossed the room and lowered onto one knee in front of Jessica, where she sat at the small table in front of the window. His eyes captured her, reflecting his sincere love for her.

"Do you really want to go? We talked about Hawaii, which would be wise this time of year; but I kinda have my heart set on Maine."

"In December."

"Precisely."

Jessica folded the newspaper as Matt approached her.

"Any particular reason?" he said.

"Yes, but I'd rather surprise you."

"Would it be safe to let you?"

Jessica stood. Matt, likewise. She smiled up at him, her blue-green eyes sparkling.

"You trust me, don't you?"

"Mostly," said Matt, still cautious.

"Well, that will have to do—for now," she said. "I can promise you one thing for sure. Our life together will never be dull."

Matt pulled Jessica closer to him.

"I love you, Jess, more than words can say. And yes, of course I trust you. Whatever it is, I'm sure we will have fun. Frozen fun, mind you—but fun, nonetheless."

Their honeymoon flight landed in Portland, Maine around 1:30 in the afternoon. God blessed them with a smooth flight and chilly, but mild weather. They would have plenty of time to enjoy the city and finish their Christmas shopping.

Matt and Jessica Baldwin slept in the next day and left the "Do Not Disturb" sign on the door until the lavishly late hour of 10:30.

"So much for breakfast," said Matt.

"Not a big loss, really," said Jessica. "By the time I get myself together, it will be time for lunch, anyway."

An hour later, the newlyweds climbed aboard the rented four-wheel-drive pickup truck equipped with snow tires and chains, and headed out to find a cozy mom-and-pop eatery. One that the locals frequented, and would offer better food than atmosphere.

"I love you, Jess," said Matt, glancing across the cab of the truck.

"I love you, too," she said, completely engrossed in the latest chapter of her life. And thoroughly excited about the way it would be launched. The timing couldn't have been better.

December third would be special for her as a journalist, and memorable for them as a couple. She couldn't contain the smile that spread across her face, or the muffled giggle that escaped her lips.

"Something funny?"

"Just giddy, I guess. All my dreams have come true."

"All of them?"

"Well, so far. Some I haven't dreamed yet. Oh!" she suddenly gasped. "Matt, look! We *have* to eat there, and find out why they named it Duckfat!"

"Okay," he said. "If it means that much to you, I'll find a parking space."

Matt found himself caught up in the enthusiasm that bubbled up from deep inside his wife. Just thinking about it made him smile. Jessica had agreed to marry him, and had actually followed through with it. His spirit resonated with hers in a gratifying way. Life and love promised to be a fruitful and adventurous journey.

He had prayed for an opportunity to have children of his own one day, an opportunity to watch them grow, graduate from high school, and maybe college, if they might be bent that way. An opportunity to enjoy grandchildren, and maybe even great grandchildren. An opportunity to make special, for his own family, all the years he had lived without a dad. Sometimes he wished his mother had married Tommy years before they actually tied the knot. Tommy was a compassionate, godly man, and would have been a good dad.

Matt pushed the memories, and the loss, and even the hopes aside, in order to focus on his bride.

As he shoved the gear-shift knob into place, he opened the driver's side door, with every intention of making his way around to open the door for Jessica. But when he looked up, she was already at the door of the restaurant, staring in the window, apparently fascinated with what she saw inside. He shook his head and made a detour away from the truck. Yep. This marriage would be an adventure. Nothing conventional about Jessica Roberts Baldwin.

Their waiter explained the simplicity of the name Duckfat. "Duckfat features classic Belgian fries made with local Maine potatoes fried in duck fat," he said.

Jessica's laugh filled the corner where they had been seated. "As simple as that," she said.

"That's right."

"Well, bring us some, please," she said. "I'd like to try them."

Matt and Jessica perused the menu and decided on a main course then set back to enjoy a leisurely half hour, taking in the sights outside the small window beside their table, engaging in conversation, and falling deeper and deeper in love.

The following day, Matt and Jessica Baldwin traveled the hour and a half to Farmington, where Matt still had no idea what to expect.

Snow fell on them all the way. By the time they arrived, an inch of fresh snow had accumulated on top of the two inches that had fallen the night before.

As they approached the entrance to the city, Matt looked over at Jessica, whose eyes were round with wonder, and her mouth agape, as she stared straight ahead.

"Jess, what is all this?"

"I think it's adorable," she said.

"What is?"

"If you'll find a place to park, I'll tell you all about it."

"Yes, ma'am," he said with a grin.

The moment Matt pushed the gear-shift into PARK, Jessica unfolded the Internet article she had been carrying in her purse since the day she had read it. With a grin, she handed it across the seat to her husband.

It read:

FARMINGTON: FRANKLIN COUNTY'S SHIRETOWN

Chester Greenwood, one of Farmington's most famous citizens, was born here, son of Zina and Emily (Fellows) Greenwood. He married Isabel Whittier and was the father of four children.

Chester's mechanical and creative ability likely came through his father's family. Zina was a bridge builder, a wagon & carriage builder and a businessman in the Corn Canning Industry. All of the boys in the family had that same tendency to the creative and the mechanical. Chester did indeed patent Ear Muffs when he was 15 years old. And before too many years passed, Chester was producing earmuffs in a factory in West Farmington. He continued production of earmuffs until his death in 1937—nearly 60 years—providing jobs for many women. Women were suited for the work because of their ability to sew.

While Farmington and the world remembers Chester for his "ear protectors", there was a lot more to Chester than that. He ran a bicycle shop—selling and repairing "wheels". He sold Florida Boilers, a business that grew rapidly. He later sold that business because he couldn't provide the service it required.

At the end of the 19th century, Chester became involved in the Telephone & Telegraph business. He owned and operated Franklin Telephone & Telegraph, which he expanded east toward New Sharon and north to the Phillips area. He later sold this business to a competitor.

Chester continued to invent and receive patents. He created a tea kettle with a special bottom. He invented an advertising match box, which he likely didn't mass produce. He built and patented a boring machine, which was used in the wood turning industry. The last thing he patented was a spring-tooth rake. He invented other things—a pipe-vise, an umbrella holder, and a portable camp. These were never patented.

He built a beautiful Victorian house for his family. It stands today. He was active in town affairs and participated in a committee to research and build better roads for the town. He was active in the Unitarian Church with his wife, Isabel. And he and Isabel were staunch supporters of the Grange.

All the while, Chester provided jobs for folks who needed work, and he invented.

He built solid buildings in Farmington Village for his businesses—he preferred brick. He had foresight in construction because his buildings had solid bases, which could be expanded. He purchased land, subdivided it, and created a new neighborhood near his home and with it, came a street that still bears his name. And he supported education, presumably because he didn't have a lot of formal education himself. All of his children attended college.

There truly was a lot more to Chester than just being the inventor of ear protectors.

Chester Greenwood

By Nancy Porter, author of "Chester...More than Ear Muffs"

Matt lowered the article and placed it on the seat between them.

"Only you," he said.

"Pretty special, don't you think?"

"I admit it is a great human interest story. You ready to find a place closer so we can watch the parade?"

Jessica didn't wait to answer (of course). She was out of the truck and tugging on thick woolen mittens and had placed a pair of zebra-striped earmuffs firmly over her ears, before he could kill the engine and get his door open.

For the next hour, they laughed together as they watched a myriad of earmuff styles, both in the parade and out, and pointed at giant earmuffs strapped over police squad cars and firetrucks. The afternoon turned sunny, and the snow glistened with each sparkling pile or individual flake that still fell, intermittently.

A glorious way to begin their new life together.